G R JORDAN

The Silent War

A Highlands and Islands Detective Thriller #46

Contents

Foreword

The events of this book, while based around real and also fictitious locations around the UK, are entirely fictional and all characters do not represent any living or deceased person. All companies are fictitious representations and locations have been modified for the purposes of the story. This novel is best read on the quiet while pretending to go about your normal business!

Acknowledgments

vi

To Ken, Jean, Colin, Evelyn, John and Rosemary for your work in bringing this novel to completion, your time and effort is deeply appreciated.

Books by G R Jordan

The Highlands and Islands Detective series (Crime)

1. Water's Edge
2. The Bothy
3. The Horror Weekend
4. The Small Ferry
5. Dead at Third Man
6. The Pirate Club
7. A Personal Agenda
8. A Just Punishment
9. The Numerous Deaths of Santa Claus
10. Our Gated Community
11. The Satchel
12. Culhwch Alpha
13. Fair Market Value
14. The Coach Bomber
15. The Culling at Singing Sands
16. Where Justice Fails
17. The Cortado Club
18. Cleared to Die
19. Man Overboard!
20. Antisocial Behaviour
21. Rogues' Gallery
22. The Death of Macleod - Inferno Book 1

Kirsten Stewart Thrillers (Thriller)

1. A Shot at Democracy
2. The Hunted Child
3. The Express Wishes of Mr MacIver
4. The Nationalist Express
5. The Hunt for 'Red Anna'
6. The Execution of Celebrity
7. The Man Everyone Wanted
8. Busman's Holiday
9. A Personal Favour
10. Infiltrator
11. Implosion
12. Traitor

Jac Moonshine Thrillers

1. Jac's Revenge
2. Jac for the People
3. Jac the Pariah

Siobhan Duffy Mysteries

1. A Giant Killing
2. Death of the Witch
3. The Bloodied Hands
4. A Hermit's Death

The Contessa Munroe Mysteries (Cozy Mystery)

1. Corpse Reviver
2. Frostbite
3. Cobra's Fang

The Patrick Smythe Series (Crime)

1. The Disappearance of Russell Hadleigh
2. The Graves of Calgary Bay
3. The Fairy Pools Gathering

Austerley & Kirkgordon Series (Fantasy)

1. Crescendo!
2. The Darkness at Dillingham
3. Dagon's Revenge
4. Ship of Doom

Supernatural and Elder Threat Assessment Agency (SETAA) Series (Fantasy)

1. Scarlett O'Meara: Beastmaster

Island Adventures Series (Cosy Fantasy Adventure)

1. Surface Tensions

Dark Wen Series (Horror Fantasy)

1. The Blasphemous Welcome
2. The Demon's Chalice

Chapter 01

DCI Seoras Macleod thought that the banks of Loch Ness had never looked more picturesque. It was chilly, but that was only because it was early morning. He had mused on the contents of the envelope given to him by Anna Hunt, not for long, but certainly through last night.

He wasn't back here to ask questions. He wasn't back here to see if he could get help. Instead, he wanted to meet with two of his closest colleagues.

Before he'd come up north, before he'd decided to be based up in Inverness, Macleod had travelled to the Isle of Lewis on a case along with Hope McGrath. He remembered it well.

Hope had been a determined young woman in a time when he was struggling with his relationships with anyone. The death of his wife had caused him damage in respect to how he saw others. Macleod had retreated into the shell of what he'd been brought up with, a dominating male perspective, a fixed idea of how everyone should live their life.

He'd been such an idiot back then, but Hope had worked with him all these years, and she was becoming everything he'd hoped she'd become. First and foremost, herself. She'd also settled with a decent man, and she was now a Detective

Inspector in the force. A clever woman, but she also understood her weaknesses, something Macleod was very aware of regarding himself. He'd passed so much on to her, but in truth, he'd also learnt from her. She was his closest colleague.

Not far behind was Kirsten. He sometimes thought she was the daughter he'd never had, but given her role within the Service, he wasn't too sure if he really wanted that mantle anymore.

Kirsten thought like him. She was sharp. She could read people. But having gone to the Service, she was also incredibly fit, fabulously agile, brutally decisive, and a capable killer when needed. It's not how he liked to think of her, but she was, and it was required at times. That was the difference between them. He could never work for the Service. Macleod caught killers. He could never execute them.

He heard the car arrive and didn't look up, and continued to sit at the wooden table looking out to the waters of Loch Ness. It was one of the deepest stretches of inland water in the United Kingdom, but he'd never seen the bottom. He'd only ever seen the top, seen the wind causing it to stir. Today, though, it was calm, and the sun was glinting off the water as it climbed above the top of the surrounding mountains.

Macleod wished the sun would hurry and warm him up. Sitting on the table beside him was a flask of coffee. Maybe he had learned that from Anna Hunt. She was clever, the head of the Service—clever because she engaged you and yet, she was as deadly, if not more so, than Kirsten. He wasn't sure of the nature of what she'd given him in the envelope, however.

Macleod had thought long and hard about handing it back and telling her to investigate. He'd seen too much already. Seen too much killing. Although he had no love for the criminal fraternity, those he had named the Revenge group, so many had died in the trap laid by the Forseti group. They had pulled the Revenge group in, slaughtering them in the Cairngorms.

Now he wasn't engaged in policing as he knew it. But then again, the Forseti group was bypassing policing. Macleod lifted his eyes up the hillside and then to the bright rays of sunshine that broke across to the far banks of Loch Ness.

'Have you been here all night?'

Macleod turned his head and gave a faint smile as he saw the bright white cheeks of his Detective Inspector. Hope McGrath was dressed in her beloved leather jacket, but it was parted more than it normally would have been. Her bump had developed to the point where it was now noticeable. Well, more than noticeable. She wasn't waddling yet, because there was still a while to go before she would give birth. But she was at a point where she shouldn't be running around?

'Sorry to drag you out,' he said.

'Junior's had me up most of the night anyway,' said Hope. She gave a pleasant smile at Macleod before she could see he was in one of those sombre moods.

'I hope that's coffee.'

Macleod smiled thinly at the smaller black-haired woman behind Hope. Although she was far from Hope's six feet and didn't have striking red hair, Kirsten Stewart was a power pack. Her figure was trim, muscular, and these days she had eyes that could cut through you. Macleod remembered her as the helpful police constable on the Isle of Lewis, delving into a cricket club and the murder associated with it. He had liked her then, as a person, and as a detective.

'Should have brought Ross,' said Hope. 'Takes me back. The four of us at the start. Do you remember?'

Macleod nodded. 'He'd probably be the one out of all of us who wouldn't be getting nostalgic about it. Yet he'd probably have a photograph on his laptop somewhere.'

Kirsten grinned. 'That was a long time ago,' she said. 'A lot of water under the bridge since then.'

'That's not why you called us out here, though,' said Hope, looking at the envelope sitting on the table.

'I think you just wanted coffee with two good-looking women,' said Kirsten, and slid onto the wooden bench of the table opposite Macleod.

'That's from Anna Hunt,' said Macleod.

Hope took a seat beside Kirsten while Macleod poured coffee. Hope was impressed when he pulled out a sachet of decaf coffee, along with some hot water in a slightly smaller flask that was hidden under the table.

'Why are we out here?' asked Hope. 'Why have you brought this out here? We have offices, loads of offices. I know you don't like the view from your window, but really?'

'The view's better here,' said Macleod.

He saw Hope give a faint grin, but Kirsten was straight on to what the real reason was.

'This'll be Anna's bait, to keep you going, to keep you investigating. But you don't want to,' said Kirsten.

'We've been targeted. Too much. And these people,' said Macleod, 'they took out the Revenge group, just like that. Without you, I could have lost Emmett, Sabine. I don't know if it's wise to go on. I don't know if I should dump this back to Anna and tell her to investigate it properly. Use the Service.'

'You once said I had your brains,' said Kirsten.

'Yes, you think like me. That's why you're here, so I know I'm thinking straight, from my perspective.'

'So what, I'm the driver?' asked Hope. 'Because, really, for a pregnant woman, that's not helpful. You're meant to treat me better than that, not just put me on chauffeur duty.'

'You're here because you don't think like me. I trust the pair of you, more than anyone else, at least in the detective world. I don't know if it's right to take this or not. If we open it, we'll have to follow it. Because if Anna's given this to me, there's something there. And it won't rest easy with me to pass it up.'

'No, it won't,' said Hope. 'You'll want to round it up. You'll want to tie up the loose ends. This may not be a case where loose ends can get tied up.'

'They may get tied up,' said Kirsten. 'But maybe not how you would like it.'

'A "silent war." That's what she called it,' said Macleod.

'She wants you to go at them. She wants you to find who the top person is,' said Kirsten. 'That's always been the remit. That's what we're doing.'

'To pull them in. To assemble a case and put them up before the law,' insisted Macleod.

'The law may not be capable of handling this lot,' said Kirsten.

'Exactly,' said Macleod. 'So, we hand it back to the Service.'

'She can't trust the Service,' said Kirsten.

'Why?' said Hope. 'I can trust my people. Implicitly. I even trust you. And you've been outside of the Service, Kirsten, outside of the force.'

'You don't understand what Anna's gone through. You people look at the Service as this sort of great vast blanket of an organisation. All quiet. Running around, solving everything underneath. It's not. It's a network of people wondering whether they can trust each other. You're able to operate in the dark, but can you operate in the dark with each other, if you get what I mean.'

'No, I don't,' said Hope.

'She means,' said Macleod, 'you're trained not to trust anyone. You're trained to second guess everything. You're trained to think about what betrayal is. We're not. We're trained to find a killer, trained to build up evidence. But we have a general trust that what we're saying is, at least in the raw facts, what actually is. When you deceive and pull the wool over people's eyes for a living, it becomes very hard to know the difference.'

'It's more than that,' said Kirsten. 'The Service was torn apart. You didn't read about it, but it was bloody. Very bloody. Anna's still working out who to trust. She wouldn't give you this lightly, Seoras.'

'Are you saying if I gave it back to her, she wouldn't be able to sort this out?'

'Well, she's handed it to you,' said Kirsten. 'This has been a tough one. She doesn't know who to trust, doesn't know who, up above, is pulling the strings and with such force. Anna's out on a limb here. She can't solve this on her own, that's why she's come to you. And she's come to you because she knows you're dogged, you're determined. But more than that, you will find the truth. You'll find the snake's head.'

'So, you're saying I don't give it back to her?' said Macleod.

'She can't afford for you to give it back to her,' said Kirsten.

'More than that, Seoras,' said Hope. 'You can't give this back. You're so deep into this now. You need to get to the bottom of it; otherwise, when you retire, which isn't that far away, this will still haunt you. You will still think about this, still be trying to solve this.'

'What makes you say that?' asked Kirsten.

'You may think like him, but he's a detective like me. Aren't you?' said Hope, smiling at Macleod. 'We solve it. We get to the bottom of it. By hook or by crook, however we do it, we get there. Open it,' said Hope.

Macleod took the envelope, broke the seal and took out a few pieces of paper and a photograph.

'What is it?' asked Hope.

Macleod studied the paper. 'It's a receipt. A receipt for garden stones. Handwritten. Plastic stones, though.' He lifted the photograph up. 'Look,' he said. 'Those stones. They look,' he showed it to Kirsten, 'like the ones that were up in the hills. The fake ones. The ones they made the circle from at Loch Lee.'

Macleod shuffled the paper and found a small handwritten note.

'That's Anna's writing,' said Kirsten, looking at it.

Macleod read what was on the sheet before putting it down and then looked up into Hope and Kirsten's expectant faces. 'Apparently, the company who made these is gone. It burned down in a fire twenty years ago. So, the owners are untraceable. The consignment of fifty of these stones was made to a small delivery company in the Tain area. The company was called Edderton Transport. A receipt was discovered in what Anna calls an undisclosed search of one of Bairstow's factories by the Service.'

'She said she would investigate on her own as well,' said Kirsten. 'So she's been doing that.'

'Anna says she can't find any trace of Edderton Transport.'

'And that's it, is it?' asked Hope. Macleod nodded and then looked out towards the water.

'Right,' he said. 'The trail's picked up again, then. All we've got to do is find Edderton Transport.'

'But how do we do it?' asked Hope.

'We're going to go quiet this time. Nobody knows about this evidence. So just us, on the quiet. I'll talk to Jim. We'll make it look like I've ditched what we're doing.'

'Good idea,' said Kirsten.

'That's why you're here,' said Macleod. 'You can help me with it. You can tell me how to stay quiet, Kirsten. You can operate with me. I'll be on leave, Hope. You'll run the office, be my liaison. Help keep everyone else in the team safe.'

'It's not that long till I go off,' said Hope. 'But if you need me to stay on a bit—'

'No, no,' said Macleod. 'But I need you to keep me on the straight and narrow with this. I don't have to tell you I've seen so much injury, so much harm to people that I'm not sure my anger won't influence me. At the moment, I don't know whether to run from this Forseti group or get my hands around the throats of all of them. I'll need you on this, Hope, not just to keep everyone else safe while I'm off, but I need you to keep me thinking straight.'

Hope reached across and took Macleod's hand. 'You're worrying me now,' she said. 'You don't talk like this.'

'I've never been played like this. I've never seen things like this. Not this bad.'

'Well,' said Hope. 'Let's get through it. Get to the end, get you back to being the plain old big boss.'

She gave him a grin, but it quickly faded into an anxious smile. Macleod let his hand slip from hers, and he picked up his coffee. She was right. He had to end it. He couldn't hand it back over.

Chapter 02

Tanya was nervous. She had spent over an hour working out what to wear. The weather was good, pleasant, maybe even warm, but she still wasn't sure. Should she go for a summer dress? Or maybe some neat jeans, maybe a t-shirt or a blouse? Did she want to look sophisticated or casual?

That was the problem with Perry. Perry didn't tell you what he wanted. He would defer all the time. Perry wanted you to be you. He never saw himself as being worth the effort of other people. He was selfless in that sense, and that was what Tanya loved about him.

You knew with Perry that you were going to get a man who was there for you. He wouldn't just disappear off. He wouldn't just get fed up of you. But the difficult side was knowing exactly what Perry wanted.

In the end, she'd gone for a skirt that was maybe slightly shorter than normal. These days, she wore nothing too short. Things were more practical. But this one stopped just about the knee. She wore a summer blouse above it and hoped that it didn't look like she was in the office. She had a gold chain around her neck that she thought emphasised it. And she had brushed her hair until she was sure it had all come out into the brush and there was probably nothing left on top.

Tanya dressed in five minutes normally, never worrying about how she looked because she always looked good. She always looked like a confident woman. But right now, she was all but a gibbering wreck. And yet, she wanted him.

Perry had avoided her recently, and she knew why. Perry was not good at decisions. Especially when he didn't want to let people down. Clearly, his colleague Susan was someone he valued. He'd saved her life, apparently. That was a connection that was hard to get past. But she was younger than him. Too young. Tanya was his age, more suited for him.

Tanya laughed at herself. Had it got so bad that the best she could do was say that she was the same age as someone? Tanya was right for Perry because Tanya was everything he could want. They'd always got on well together, and she'd moved up here for him. He'd wanted it.

She could tell because he hadn't told her she had got the wrong idea. And Perry would. Perry would do that straight away. He wouldn't want somebody put out because of him. And yet he was struggling now to make a choice. But he had decided to meet her.

Tanya stood on the side of the Caledonian Canal, near to where it broke out towards the River Ness. They hired small cruisers close to here and she parked her car down by those offices. After a short walk, she had sat down on a bench. She then texted Perry exactly where she was. Now, she saw him approaching.

He was shuffling along. *Poor man*, she thought. *He's not looking forward to this.* She could tell he was conflicted.

Perry was wearing a pair of beige trousers, a shirt, and a

jacket over the top. He approached Tanya as if he didn't quite want to reach her, but would rather keep at a distance. But as he did so, Perry lifted his eyes and beamed.

'Glad you're here,' said Tanya.

'You look great,' he said, and then fell silent.

'Shall we walk?'

'Yes,' said Perry, 'good idea.'

Tanya took up a pace, but it was gentle, and Perry walked beside her.

'There's been a lot of pressure lately on people.'

'Yes,' said Perry, 'the cases have been difficult. I think Seoras has kept you out of most of it. To be honest, you don't really want to know.'

'Well, I've seen bits and pieces. He's been under a lot of stress. You must be too.'

'Part of the job,' said Perry almost dismissively. But she could tell it was getting to him.

'I understand,' said Tanya. 'I understand the situation you're in.' Perry gave her a quizzical look. 'You aren't good at hiding things.'

'Hiding what?' said Perry.

'Perry, you came to me in Glasgow and, well, it was obvious. It was obvious you were thinking about where we'd been before. So was I. That day when I saw you come in, you lit me up again. I was also sorry you left Glasgow. I never wanted you to leave. Especially when I became single, I regretted my choices. But I took a chance. I came up here. I came up here to spend time with you. To find out if there was something between us, Perry. Something that could be longer term.'

'I know you did,' said Perry.

'And as much as this case has taken its toll on you . . . you have been avoiding me.'

'I wouldn't avoid you,' said Perry.

'Warren, you've been avoiding me. I'm not stupid.'

'What do you mean?'

'Don't do that,' she said. 'You know as well as I do. You've got feelings for Susan, and I don't blame you. Annoyingly, she's a lovely girl. Really is. She's super. I hate to say that,' said Tanya. 'She's also younger than me.'

'Whoa,' said Perry. 'Age doesn't come into this.'

'So, you admit it. You have feelings for her.'

Perry stopped walking for a moment. 'Yes,' he said. 'And I have feelings for you. But . . .'

'But?' said Tanya.

'It's hard,' said Perry.

'What's hard is that you spend most of your time with her. I don't get a fair look in. Yes? You're not giving me a fair shout. I need time with you. You get that, don't you?'

'There's not been a lot of time,' said Perry. 'With detectives, this is what happens. You are all on the go and suddenly—'

'Don't talk to me about how people within the force work. I was HR in the force for how long? Dammit, Perry, I know how people work. Don't give me that trite nonsense. Warren Perry, it's the last I'd expect from you.'

'Sorry,' said Perry.

Tanya hated herself for those words. If you got him right, if you called him out, Perry didn't even begin to defend himself. And you loved him all the more for it.

Tanya put her hand up to Perry's cheek. 'I'm up here because I think the world of you, Perry.'

Tanya suddenly saw that Perry was looking beyond her.

'Are you listening to me?' she said. And Perry nodded. 'You

could at least react. You could at least give me something here. What's a girl meant to do? You need to pick. You need to make a decision, Perry. Perry, would you look at me when I'm talking to you?'

Perry's eyes were over her shoulder. And then suddenly he looked back down the canal.

'You can't avoid me like that,' said Tanya. 'You can't do that to me. I've come all the way up to Inverness. I have moved my life. To be here, because I thought this was a chance. Dammit, Perry, would you listen to me?'

For a moment, he looked back at her. And then he looked up the canal again. And then he looked around him. He was getting nervous. She could see the sweat forming on his brow.

'You have to decide. Pick one of us and try to make it work. That's what you need to do. It's only fair, Perry. It's not fair you hold me here. You pick her, fine. You won't want me around, fine. I'll get out of the way. But I can't stand every day coming into that office not knowing whether you're thinking of her, thinking of me, or what you're doing. It's killing me, Perry. It's killing me and it's not fair to me. You must understand; it's not fair to me. Would you bloody well look at me? Look at me, you stupid man!'

Once again, Perry's eyes were everywhere else. 'Do I need to bloody well hit you? Perry!' Tanya reached forward, grabbed Perry by the cheeks, and tried to turn his head towards her. But it didn't budge. He looked down the canal behind Tanya.

Without warning, he put his hands around, grabbed her hips, and picked her up. They were only four feet from the canal, and Perry took a running jump and launched the pair of them into it. Tanya's head was slung round, briefly looking back up the canal. There was a cruiser coming now, and Perry had jumped right in front of it. They hit the water, just on the far side of it. Perry's shoulder was clipped by the boat, and pushed him further away into the middle of the canal. The cold water chilled Tanya, but she could feel Perry holding her tight, keeping her above water, while the cruiser stopped beside them.

'What the bloody hell are you doing? What are you up, man?'

Perry wasn't watching the angry helmsman. He was looking to either side.

'Get out of the water. You need to get out,' said the helmsman. He reached down into the water, and Perry pushed Tanya towards the man's hands. As she went to get up, hauled out of the water by the man, Perry said, 'Stay low. Don't get up. Lie on the deck.'

'What the hell are you on about?' said the man.

'Tanya, do it!'

The man reached over, pulled Perry up, while Tanya lay on the deck. She saw Perry roll onto the deck, but not stand up. Instead, he stayed low and crawled round to the side of the cruiser and looked down the canal. Then he looked up the other way.

'Is your friend okay? He's lost it,' said the helmsman.

Tanya went to stand up, but Perry held his hand out, indicating she should stay low. He continued to look for a couple of minutes before he motioned her to stand. Clearly, something was wrong. She walked over to him and put a hand on his shoulder.

'Sorry,' said Perry.

'What is it?' asked Tanya.

'Something's up,' he said. She put her hand into his and found he was trembling. She wasn't sure it was from the cold or having been in the water. He was now looking back down the canal, and she could see a woman running along the path. The woman screamed.

'What's up?' asked Perry, shouting from the cruiser.

The woman started pointing into the water. Tanya stood, looking over Perry's shoulder, down into the water to see something was floating towards them. As it got closer, she recognised the shape.

'Oh, hell,' said Perry. 'That's a body.'

Perry turned to the helmsman, asking if he had a hook or something. The man disappeared inside the cruiser's cabin before coming back with an extendable pole, which did indeed have a hook on the end. Perry reached into the water with it.

Aided by the man, Perry hooked onto some of the clothing of the body. He pulled it close and told the man to tie his cruiser up alongside the canal. Once he was sure he had secured the body against the cruiser, Perry reached for his phone.

'Will it still work?' asked Tanya.

'Wasn't in for that long,' said Perry. 'This one should do.'

She watched him place a call into the station before explaining to the helmsman of the boat that he was a Detective Constable with the local police. This quietened the man down. Tanya could see he was struggling to process the events.

Perry stepped ashore and went to the woman who had pointed out the body. She was still hysterical, shouting out every now and again and pointing down. A small crowd was forming, and it was another ten minutes before the first police car arrived. It was another ten after that, before the scene was vaguely secure, and Perry came over to Tanya. As he approached, she felt stupid. Clearly, something had gone down, something she hadn't seen, and she'd been berating him.

'I'm sorry,' she said, 'I was just angry, I was . . .'

Perry took hold of her shoulders and pulled her close to him. He kissed her on the forehead.

'Thank God you're okay,' he said. Then he wrapped his arms around her and held her close.

Chapter 03

Macleod watched as Hope parked the car, then had to swing herself out of it to stand up. He realised the bump was starting to get in the way. As she got out to the other side, she turned to look at him.

'You don't have to stare,' she said. 'I know it's awkward, but I am getting close. A few more months and I won't be able to sit anywhere.'

'A few more months you'll be sitting, holding that one in your hands, instead of carrying them around in your belly,' said Macleod. 'You know you can go any time. You know you can take the time.'

'You need me at the moment,' said Hope. 'And I need to see this through, too. It's how you and I are the same.' Macleod nodded and strolled with her along the canal bank before showing his credentials to a uniformed police officer. They made their way up towards where a cruiser was moored at the side of the canal.

Jona Nakamura was there, the forensic lead for the station. As Macleod approached, she held up a hand, indicating he should keep his distance. He stood waiting for a couple of minutes before Jona made her way over, pulling down the hood on her forensic coverall. The diminutive Asian woman looked somewhat perplexed.

'What's the matter?' asked Macleod.

'A bit confused by what happened.'

'I take it the victim was drowned,' said Macleod.

'No, no,' said Jona. 'The victim was stabbed by a professional.'

'Down here,' said Macleod.

'Somewhere up the canal, somewhere up there. Probably dropped into the river, floated down to here from what I can gather, pulled into the canal side by Perry and the master of that boat,' she said.

'Stabbed by a professional?' queried Hope.

'A proper kill. This is somebody who knows how to kill, quick, efficient, no messing, dead by the time she hit the water.'

'Any more detail?' asked Macleod.

'It's just a summation at the moment. I need to get her back onto the table and have a proper look, but it seems to me what happened was a very professional hit.'

Macleod looked around. 'Bright day. Why take her out here? I mean, we don't even know who she is.'

'She's got ID on her,' said Jona. 'Also a gun inside her jacket.'

'What type of gun?' asked Macleod.

'Small handgun, silencer too.' Macleod looked at Hope.

'Our friend here?' asked Hope.

'Not that I've seen,' said Jona, referring to Anna Hunt. 'I've seen nothing from anyone outside of ourselves.'

'Where's Perry?' asked Macleod.

'One of the ambulances is over there. Bit shaken up, to say the least. So's Tanya.'

'Tanya?' said Macleod.

'Tanya was here with him. That's why he was here. Perry

called it in.'

'What?' said Macleod.

'Perry called it in.'

'Thank you,' said Macleod, and walked directly over to the ambulance, leaving Hope in his wake. Only when he got there, and was going to climb into the back of it, did he turn to assist her.

'Sorry,' he said. 'Should have thought.'

Hope ignored him. Stepping into the back of the ambulance, they saw Perry lying down. Tanya was in the seat nearby. A paramedic was checking Perry out, but there was another one there, with her back to Macleod. He recognised the figure though. Trim, long black hair, currently pulled into a ponytail. He turned to Hope.

'Close the door,' he said. She did so without question, and then Macleod said, 'I take it this has got something to do with you.'

'I don't know it's got anything to do with me,' said Perry. 'I just came down—'

'I'm not talking to you, Perry. Sorry,' said Macleod. 'Anna?'

The paramedic with the black ponytail turned and gave Macleod a faint smile. 'It's not to do with me,' she said. 'It's just that the body you've pulled from the canal is one of mine. One of mine looking after Tanya.'

'I'm sorry,' said Macleod.

'Yes, well, the thing is that my people don't go down easy.'

'From what Jona tells me,' said Macleod, 'it looks like she was taken out quickly, very professionally.'

'Would have had to have been an excellent operator,' said Anna.

'So, what happened?' asked Macleod.

'Perry saw them. Perry's seen them! Perry . . .'

Macleod turned to Tanya. She was shaking. He knelt down beside her, taking her hands. 'Easy,' he said. 'Easy. Let Perry talk. You're okay now. You're in good hands.' He continued to hold her hands while he looked over at Perry.

'We were here to meet, and we were walking, and then I just clocked two people coming. One from either side. It didn't look right, really didn't look right. Something about the way they moved, focused on me too much. People don't look at me,' said Perry. 'I'm just not that guy. There's nothing dramatic about me. So when people start looking, I start thinking that something's up. Then I realised,' said Perry, 'that they weren't looking just at me. They were looking at Tanya too.'

Macleod could hear Tanya beginning to weep more, and ignoring his normal protocols, he wrapped her up in a hug. 'It's fine, you're okay,' he said. 'You're good.'

'That poor woman,' said Tanya.

'I saw them coming,' said Perry, 'and I just grabbed Tanya and threw her and me into the canal. There was a cruiser coming. And I thought that if I got to the other side of it, it would shield me.'

'He got caught by the cruiser,' said Anna. 'Hit him on the shoulder. That's why he's in here.'

'However,' said the other paramedic, a blonde-haired woman in her late thirties, 'it's just a bruise, there's nothing seriously damaged.'

'She's one of mine,' said Anna, pointing to the paramedic. 'But she's a proper paramedic within the Service.'

Macleod nodded. 'I won't ask your name, but thank you,' he said.

'By the looks of it, if Perry hadn't got to the other side of that cruiser, we could have been talking a different story. Public Place, their initial plan, got blown,' said Anna.

'Worse?' said Tanya, all of a sudden.

'Hope,' said Macleod. Can you—' he pointed to Tanya.

Hope stepped forward. When Macleod stepped aside, she embraced Tanya again.

'Anna, can we talk outside?' asked Macleod.

Anna nodded and followed Macleod out to the side of the ambulance. 'How did you get one of these?' he asked once they were outside the ambulance.

'We have protocols and ways to get on to things,' she said. 'Don't worry about that now. This was close, Seoras. Too close.'

'By the sounds of it, Perry saved their lives.'

'Very quick thinking. Brilliant, actually,' said Anna. 'I'm very impressed by him. Especially for someone with a bit of bulk.'

'I'm sorry for your colleague.'

'I have people around. To get past them is not easy. They're not all of Kirsten's or my standard, but they're not slack. I don't employ slack people.'

'Regarding your evidence, I'm looking into it.'

'Can I suggest a subtle shift?' said Anna.

'What do you mean?' asked Macleod.

'Well, so far, you've been investigating with your teams out and about. I would get your people back to looking like they're doing normal work. Get Jim to call off the task force. Then you do this on your own. We say you need time off. You've had a heck of a tough time. Take Perry. He had a rough time here too. I'll get Tanya out of the way. Get her far away from Inverness, and get your Jane to go with her,' said Anna. 'Somewhere I can keep them very safe. Not out and about. Every reason to get

Tanya out of the way. You can be on holiday with Jane.'

'And do what? Run this investigation by not being there?'

'It's safest for them. Of course you'll still be here.'

'I had been thinking along those lines.'

'It's getting to a head, Seoras. We've knocked at the door so many times about this. We've got close. I don't need you to get them into a court. I need to know who it is.'

'I'm a police officer,' said Macleod.

'I need that police officer brain,' said Anna. 'I don't need the police officer lecture.'

'Have you really no way to do this yourself?' asked Macleod.

'I'm here, aren't I? I'm handing it to you. You don't think I choose to use you because I just thought it was a pleasant option. As much as I enjoy meeting with you, as much as I enjoy your company,' said Anna, in a way that actually scared Macleod that she really did, 'I wouldn't do that to someone. If the Service could handle this, I would handle it. We can't. I don't have the trust. I can't bring Kirsten back in because that would be a red flag to everyone. While she's with you, if anyone sees her, she's rogue. And that suits us. She will keep you safe.'

'They came for Tanya,' said Macleod. 'What's to stop them from coming for anyone else?'

'I will get on it,' said Anna.

'You were on it. One of your people died.'

'One of the problems now that the Forsetis have got rid of the Revenge group, and the added self-destruction of the Macintoshes, is that the resources of the Forseti group can now be aimed at their greatest enemy. This has changed recently. It used to be the Macintoshes, it used to be the Revenge group coming for them. After all, they were cutting into their organisation. They aren't there anymore. The biggest threat to Forseti Group, as they see it, is you and your people.'

'And not you,' said Macleod.

'No, because the Service isn't involved in that way. I have a bit more latitude and I can play my cover a lot better,' said Anna. 'Besides, you're too good, you're too true to what a detective is, to what a police officer should be. They know you won't quit. Everyone knows you won't quit. It's what scares them. It's what's making them come for you. Tanya, soft target. Too easy. Perry, much harder.

'Let me take Tanya away. Take Jane away too. I'll get better cover on the other families, but your team looks like it is back working normally. They won't suspect them. At least, I hope not.'

'And so, I follow this evidence that you've given me.'

'Yes. I'll step in here,' said Anna. 'It's one of my people. I'll take care of this death. I'll say it's Service business. We'll step in and make it okay. You investigate on the quiet. Tell Jim you're on holiday.'

'Okay,' said Macleod. 'But I'm trusting you. You need to protect my people.'

'Seoras,' she said firmly, but quietly. 'I will protect them as best I can. I have just lost one of my people out there. And you may think I'm a cold-hearted bitch, but I'm not. That young woman out there has two brothers and a father that won't see her again. At some point, I will speak to them and tell them that. I have my people too. I will defend yours as best I can, but I suggest you follow the evidence and you do it quickly and quietly. And get me something to go on.'

Macleod nodded. He went to turn away, but Anna grabbed his hand. Pulling him back, she kept hold of it.

'I didn't want to put this on you. It's not fair. It's not right. But I need someone I can trust, and I need someone who's good enough. Kirsten doesn't have the other resources. She can't do this alone. Take her with you. She'll be incredibly useful. She's used to investigating in a way where we, well . . . we cover our tracks in a rather blunt way.'

'Communicate through Hope,' said Macleod. 'She'll stay in the office. She'll be my link. I'll bring Perry with me. Others as I need them.'

'Don't dawdle on this. They seem to have got in their head that you are the problem. Your team is a problem. The safest way for me to protect your team is to know who's coming for them. You find that out for me and I'll solve it.'

Macleod turned away. He wasn't happy with that answer. But at the moment, he didn't have any other answers and his team was clearly under threat.

Chapter 04

Macleod heard the doorbell and walked to the front door, checking through the peephole. Being satisfied that a red-headed woman was standing outside, he opened the door and welcomed Hope in, taking her leather jacket off her and hanging it up.

'She's not here,' he said. 'I thought it best that Jane go sooner rather than later.'

'Probably wise. I've been worried about John, but we've got another couple of people about the place. I wasn't sure what to tell him. He hasn't spotted Anna's protection yet.'

'Anna will do her best,' said Macleod. 'Meanwhile, we're going to go out to the patio at the back. Can I get you a drink or something?'

'You're okay,' she said, but she stopped and turned to him. 'Before the others are here,' she said, 'you take care of yourself on this one. Perry and Tanya were too close. Thank God he was so watchful.'

'Thank God indeed,' said Macleod. 'We've got ourselves into something this time, and I'm not sure how to get us out of it.'

'You will,' said Hope. 'You will. I wish I could come with you. Look at me. What use am I at the moment?'

'You're always of use. Kirsten's great,' said Macleod. 'But if I have a choice, I'd have you beside me every time.'

'You're just trying to butter me up now,' said Hope, giving a smile. 'Seriously, though, you watch yourself.'

'Kirsten will watch me,' said Macleod. 'I'll get this done.' The pair made their way out to the patio, where Macleod got a seat for Hope.

While they waited for others to arrive, they talked about how Hope was doing. She said the sickness was not as bad as it had been. Her hand lingered, rolling around her belly.

'You getting kicks now?' asked Macleod. 'I heard they kick.'

'Oh, they kick,' she said. 'In fact, come here.'

She took his hand and rolled down her pregnancy jeans so that her belly was exposed. The significant bump was white, contrasting with the dark of her jeans. She took Macleod's hand, placing it onto her belly. She shivered as his hand touched.

'And when does it . . .'

'Shush, Seoras,' said Hope. 'Just wait.' Together, they sat there. And after about a minute, Macleod felt a sudden tap on his hand.

'That was the wee one?'

Hope smiled. 'Oh, that was Junior. Feels even more different on the inside.'

He continued to hold his hand there, and there was another one. 'I envy you,' he said. 'I never had this.'

'Well, if you got pregnant, that would be quite a surprise,' said Hope.

'No, I don't mean that. I mean, John must love this, to sit with you, to feel that little life.'

'You all right?' said Hope. 'You look a little emotional.

I'm not used to you being emotional. Grumpy, yes, but not emotional.'

Macleod could feel his eyes welling. 'Yes,' he said. 'I'm a little emotional.'

Hope took his hand off and pulled her pregnancy jeans back up. 'Best we not let the others see you being emotional,' she said. He leaned forward and kissed her on the forehead.

'You be so very careful,' he said.

'Am I breaking a moment?' said a voice. 'I'm sorry, if I am.'

Perry was approaching the patio from the side of the house. He was dressed in black.

'Are you okay?' asked Macleod.

'I'm all right,' he said. 'Tanya's away.'

'Anna's taken her. It's for the best,' said Macleod.

'I guess so,' said Perry. 'We kind of have a bit of unfinished business, though.'

Macleod looked beyond Perry and could see Emmett arriving. He was dressed in jeans and a jumper with what looked like a Valkyrie on it. Macleod was mystified as to how women fought in such bare outfits. But this wasn't the time for that, and he noticed Emmett had someone with him. Stumbling through the dark, but dressed in her trews and tartan shawl, Clarissa was helped onto the patio by Emmett.

'Did I really have to sneak in here?' said Clarissa.

'You did,' said Macleod. 'Thank you all for coming. Take a seat.'

'What's wrong with the office?' asked Emmett.

'Beginning to wonder how much we trust people,' said Macleod.

'Trust?' said Emmett. 'We're not getting paranoid, are we?'

Macleod shook his head. 'The threat level's gone up on

ourselves. Someone tried to take Tanya out. If it hadn't been for Perry, she'd probably be dead. They took out Anna Hunt's guard. That's how good they were.'

'Bastards,' said Clarissa.

Macleod raised his eyebrows but pointed to a chair on the patio. 'Take a seat.' Clarissa sat down and Emmett stood beside her, while Perry also stood.

'We're just waiting for one more,' said Macleod.

'She's been here all along,' said a voice, and Kirsten stepped out of the dark. She was dressed in black jeans, a black leather jacket with a black t-shirt underneath, her hair tied up. Kirsten strode into the middle of the group, before sitting down on the patio floor.

'I can get you a seat if you want,' said Macleod.

'No,' said Kirsten. 'We're clear. No one about. Let's go. Get on with what we need to do.'

'Okay,' said Macleod. 'I've brought you here because, well, you're my three heads. Kirsten because of the abilities she brings, and Perry because he's about to be tasked.'

Everyone looked towards Perry. He gave a quizzical look back.

'Don't worry,' said Macleod, 'it's not that bad. We're going back to normal investigations. Jim's going to get the word out that we've given up our particular pursuit.'

'Who's going to believe that?' asked Clarissa.

'Well, we're going to play it as best we can. However, I'm going to go on holiday, off with Jane. Jane, however, has already gone. She's being cared for along with Tanya, somewhere secret by Anna Hunt. I don't even know where she is. Kirsten and Perry will investigate some new information Anna's given me. We are going dark. Hope will be my contact.

That being said, we will keep communication to a minimum. Officially, Perry will be recuperating. You're going to go off on a break somewhere to do that.'

'Oh, right,' said Perry. 'Recuperation. Where are we going, anyway?'

'Anna, through some searches she did of Bairstow's properties, has come across a receipt. The plastic stones that were in the Forseti ring out in the Cairngorms, seem to be linked to this receipt from a while back. The company that supplied them is defunct. However, they used a transport company near Edderton. We're going to see if it still exists, or if it existed, and we're going to chase up through that line of attack because beyond that, we have nothing. Anna Hunt is asking us to do this because she doesn't trust her own people at the moment, or rather she doesn't know who to trust.'

'So, the rest of us just go back to work,' said Clarissa.

'Basically,' said Macleod; 'if I need any of you, I will call you in. Hope's the boss.'

'Well, for a couple of months,' said Clarissa. 'You'll need someone else after that.'

'There's always Emmett,' said Macleod under his breath and saw Clarissa looking over. 'This is not a rejection of any of you,' said Macleod. 'Understand that. The reason I'm doing this is that I need to do it quickly and quietly. You are at risk. Anna has put out greater protection now around you. Frank has already almost succumbed. Tanya and Perry were attacked,' said Macleod, 'and we have to be extremely careful. If we just sit back, if we run this normally, it's my belief, and Hope's, that we will get nowhere and we may lose some of us before we even manage that. The way I can protect my team is to go out and solve this.'

'If you're going rogue with it,' said Clarissa, 'I'm available. I've gone rogue before.'

'I'm aware of that,' said Macleod.

'We also need to be quiet and considered when doing this,' said Kirsten. 'It's not your forte.'

'Kirstie, dear, you've worked with me before. You know I get the job done.'

'Seoras is right with what to do at the moment. Perry has got the perfect opportunity to come with us, given what's just happened,' said Kirsten. 'Therefore, we follow this plan. You need to go back to work and make it look like nothing's happening.'

Macleod could see Clarissa wasn't happy. He looked at Hope, who raised her eyebrows.

'All I want is to get back to normal investigating,' said Macleod. 'This can't go on. It's been too much.'

'When are we getting a new ACC?' asked Clarissa. 'We're a bit exposed in the line. No ACC, no you.'

'I can handle it,' said Hope.

'For a couple of months and then you're away,' spat Clarissa.

'Jim's picking that roll up for the moment. He'll need to interview for the full-time post,' said Macleod.

'Is that it?' said Emmett. 'It's just that, given what you've said, we probably shouldn't hold this meeting for any longer than needs be.' He turned to Hope. 'Do you need any help getting back?'

'She's fine,' said Kirsten. 'She came over in the car. Everybody else came secretly. Perfectly normal for Hope to visit Seoras.'

'Very good,' said Emmett. He walked over and put his hand out to Clarissa. 'Let's get back then,' he said. Clarissa took

Emmett's hand and he helped her up out of her seat. But before she disappeared, she turned to Macleod.

'Be careful.' And then she turned to Kirsten. 'Kirstie, dear, you make sure you look after him.' Clarissa didn't wait for a response. She simply walked off, with Emmett following her quickly into the dark.

'Got to get going,' said Hope, and Macleod helped her out of her seat. He followed her through to the front door, where she hugged him and kissed his forehead. She told him once again to take care and then disappeared off to her car.

Macleod returned to the patio, where Perry and Kirsten were now sitting in chairs.

'So how does this work?' asked Perry.

'You go back tonight. Tomorrow, you'll be signed off. You'll go down to this Travel Agent. You'll book with them and then you'll disappear off in your car. Leave it at the airport. I will pick you up. You will come with me. Somebody with your name will be on the flight. After that, for the next two weeks, you're with us. You'll be changing your looks as well.'

'Very good,' said Perry.

'I realise I haven't given you a choice with this,' said Macleod. 'But to be honest, I haven't really had a choice either. Although Anna was very impressed. Your awareness saved Tanya's life.'

'You don't have to ask,' said Perry. 'Somebody went for Tanya. They could go for any of us next time. But they could go for her again. Let's put an end to it. That's what you want to do, isn't it?' Macleod nodded. 'Well, let's put an end to it. Whatever it takes.'

'Whatever it takes,' said Kirsten.

'Whatever it takes,' said Macleod in a hushed voice and he wondered what that meant. Life was never 'whatever it takes.'

It was always doing the right thing. Would this require more than that? Would he have a choice? Perry disappeared, and Macleod said he would see Kirsten tomorrow.

'Oh, I am not going anywhere,' she said. 'My bag's right there in the dark. I'm sleeping at yours tonight.'

Macleod looked at her quizzically.

'Starts now, I'm not looking after anybody else. I'm protecting you. So, I stay the night. Don't worry, I won't tell Jane.'

Chapter 05

Macleod stared across the room at Perry, sitting upright in the chair and looking a little perturbed. Ahead of Perry was a mirror, which he was gazing intently into, and wondering why his hair was very white.

'You don't think it's too white? I don't look too old, do I?'

'I'm going to put some grey in it,' said Kirsten. 'You'll look good, trust me.'

Macleod was almost laughing, except the seriousness of the situation stopped him. They'd been so long working against the Forseti group that now his people were known. He was known. These precautions were sensible.

Unlike Kirsten, who was good at handling herself, if anyone attacked, Macleod and Perry would struggle, especially against professionals. Even Anna Hope's woman had struggled against professionals. He thought for a moment about her. He never knew her. She'd never known Perry or Tanya, and yet the woman had paid for it with her life. She died protecting them, and in such a cold and abrupt way.

He thought about Anna having to tell her next of kin. In that way, it was no different to his job. You still had to see the faces. You still had to pass on that horrible news. It was hard enough, Macleod thought, when you were talking to a relative of a murder victim. He didn't even know them, and it still choked him.

'I'm going to get the clippers for you, Seoras.'

'What?' said Macleod.

'I'm going to get the clippers. Bit of a beard on you, too.'

'Clippers? My hair's quite neat, it is.'

'I didn't say it wasn't neat. What I said was I'm going to get the clippers,' announced Kirsten again. Perry stood up, having just been dismissed, and walked over to a separate chair. 'You don't think it's too white, do you?' he said to Macleod.

'I can see why you're the bombshell,' said Macleod, 'with all these women after you.'

Perry rolled his eyes at him, but there was a weariness to it. Macleod stepped over to the wooden chair Perry had vacated, and sat upright as Kirsten arrived back in the room to plug in a set of clippers. She took out one of the small guides to attach to the end. Macleod glared at it. 'Small one, isn't it? What number is that?'

'Two.'

'Two? I never have a two. Jane wouldn't like me with a number two.'

'Jane will not see you until this is done. It's not about what you like. It's about keeping your identity secret.'

With that, Kirsten switched on the clippers, and Macleod sat there while she let them roam over his head. By the time she'd finished, Macleod was as shorn as he'd ever been. She then reached inside another box, and then began to put a beard on him. It was greying, and by the end of it, he was looking in the mirror and wondering who he was. A few other marks here and there, and Macleod could have been someone else.

'I got you some clothes as well. That's yours over there,' she said to Macleod. He saw a pair of jeans, old t-shirts, polo shirts, and a loose jacket.

'Didn't they have any proper shirts?' he said.

'You ever worn anything like that?' asked Kirsten.

'Never,' he said. 'I wouldn't be seen dead in them.'

'Well, let's hope you won't be,' said Kirsten.

Perry, on the other hand, had a smart pair of shoes. And everything about him said he was a well-kept, neat man.

'Now you need to pull this off, Perry. I'm going with your politeness. Be a bit sharp with people, though, at times. That'll help the cover. And act like you own the clothes. Not your usual slouch around.'

'Me and slouching do well,' said Perry. 'I take your point.'

'Mind you do,' said Kirsten. 'It's important.'

An hour later, the three were travelling in a car to the small village of Edderton, north of Inverness, to see if they could find out about Edderton transport.

'You're the detectives, so you get out and ask the questions. I'll be about,' said Kirsten. 'I just want to make sure nobody's around you. Intercept them before they get a chance. There shouldn't be. They shouldn't know where we are. But no risks.'

Perry and Macleod got out and Perry brandished a clipboard. Macleod went to get a notebook, but Perry shook his head.

'You need to be lazy, shall we say, Seoras. And also, you're not Seoras. It doesn't work with this get-up. You can be Ollie. I'll be Donald, okay?' Macleod nodded, if a little unsure, and the pair started round the houses in the small village.

'What are we going to ask them?' said Perry.

'We can be from a heritage firm. People looking to see about transport back in the day,' said Macleod.

'And we heard of Edderton Transport then?' said Perry.

'That's the one,' said Macleod. 'Keep it there, keep it light. Maybe start off with, "Do you know of any transport that used to be here?"'

They approached the first house and found that it belonged to a couple of newlyweds who hadn't lived in Edderton for long, so they moved on. In fact, it was about four houses later when they found someone, not just of an appropriate age, but who'd also lived in the village for an appropriate amount of time.

'We're just wondering,' said Perry, 'about transport. People used to move things from this village. We're thinking of removal firms, haulage, stuff like that. We're from a group who's cataloguing old style movements throughout the country. It's an attempt to look at the lost roots of where we came from. It seems that everything nowadays is so big, you don't get so many of the small guys, except for these people chugging out the Amazon parcels.'

'And they've got their own vans,' said a woman.

'Yes,' said Perry. 'Do you remember any van companies around here?'

'There was two. Bosnicks. Bosnicks or something they called one. He wasn't very good. Bit of a gimmick to him. Didn't last long. The one before that, that was here for a while. Very low key. And he was Edderton. Remember that because he based it on here because nobody else had.'

'Edderton. Is that the full name of the company?' asked Perry.

'No, no, no. It's Edderton Transport. They weren't a big firm. They did a lot of smaller jobs. The sort that kept going, well, because, well, they did anything they could put their hands to, you know? It's what you had to do in those days. It's what a lot of people nowadays don't do. Just pick up the work where it is.'

'But where was it based?' asked Macleod, over Perry's shoulder.

'Ollie, would you give the woman a chance?' said Perry. 'I'm sorry, it's quite rude cutting across you.'

'Oh, not at all. Down the way there. It's not there anymore, though. That was the thing. It wasn't a local lad that did it. The man came into the village and was quite enterprising. American. And that southern drawl they have. Like Elvis.'

'They looked like Elvis,' said Perry, with a big smile on his face.

'Only in the latter years, quite a fat man,' said the woman. 'Didn't look that well, either. Was like Elvis, I guess.'

'But did he sing like Elvis, that's the question,' laughed Perry. Macleod didn't get it, wondering what Perry was going on about but he stood back as he saw the woman warm to Perry.

'Edderton Transport with Leo Jolly,' she said. 'Now Leo used to live about five doors down, but he's long gone from here. Quite sad, really. He lived in the village, well, for a number of years. And he had this big van, doing jobs on the side. But he died, unfortunately. A pity, because like I say, he wasn't a bad guy at all. I liked the American drawl. Louisiana, places like that. Got the feeling he was from somewhere down there. You know, the scorching sun, sitting out watching the dusk happen.'

'You say he died? What happened?'

'Oh, it was terrible. He died in his van. It was an enormous shock to everybody here. Well, you won't find many people nowadays who remember him.'

'Did he have kids?'

'Yes, there was one. I can't remember, exactly. He did have a kid. Something happened because he didn't have a wife with him. He had several girlfriends at the time, but not a wife. No. No, I can't remember anymore,' she said.

Macleod went to press, but felt Perry pushing back at his stomach. 'Well, that's really useful. Thanks very much,' said Perry.

When they left the driveway and moved down towards the next house, Macleod whispered in Perry's ear, 'I hope you've got a good reason for stopping me from talking.'

'You were about to press, Seoras. Don't press. We're here finding out about trucks, not about what happened to people when they died and who their children were. They find it suspicious. You're not a police officer when you go to the door. It's the way you get in with people. And besides, if he was no one within the village, and she said there was only a couple more here who would know him, well, they might be here still. We can always go back to her. I don't want to blow our chances.'

Macleod felt like he had been chastised, and he fell into step beside Perry. He thought Perry had made a mistake, though, until they met some of the other inhabitants.

A woman said, 'Oh yes, Leo Jolly. Well, I have to say, he was a jolly guy. Fun man. Leo and I, well, we shared a couple of nights together.' The woman was laughing. 'In fact,' she said, 'that's why the husband left me in the end. Anyway, it was a more fun way to get rid of him.'

'And what happened to Mr Jolly?' asked Perry.

'Passed on. Accident in his van. Terrible. I was at the funeral. He's buried far from here. Simple stone.'

'Would there be any family to talk to?' asked Perry. 'See if I can get any more details about his business from them.'

'Well, there was only the boy. I mean, I felt for the boy—no mum. Struggled with a number of things. Now his name . . . oh, what was it? Simon. Simon Jolly.'

'What happened to Simon?' asked Perry, putting his clipboard to one side and smiling.

'Simon? Well, we all wondered what the council would do for him, but he got taken in by an orphanage. It's not that far from here, I don't think. Well, I say not that far. It's not a hundred miles, but it's still quite a bit.'

'And how did that happen?'

'Well, he was going to be sent off to somewhere within Inverness or probably further afield. I'm not sure about what the orphanage who took him in, who they were. Private one, from what people said at the time. Never really heard of it. The name was funny, you know. It's like one of those startups, what they call them, isn't it? Or actually, even more like a church. It was something to do with fruit. Apple. Appleseed. That was it. Appleseed Orphanage. Simon Jolly went to Appleseed Orphanage.'

'And you know where it is?' asked Perry.

'Like I say, not exactly. I'm sure it must be in something. It would be in a directory, won't it? It'll have a phone number. If it's still going, of course, because Simon Jolly wouldn't be a young man anymore. He'd be a lot older. He'd be heading towards his forties, maybe? Would that be right?'

'Well, thanks for your help,' said Perry. He turned and walked with Macleod to outside the village, to where Kirsten had parked the car. Macleod put a call in to her, and she soon joined him there.

'What did you find out?' asked Kirsten.

'It was here. Edderton Transport. Long gone. Leo Jolly, an American, ran it. Died in an accident in his van.'

'How very convenient,' said Kirsten.

'Isn't it,' said Macleod. 'Appleseed Orphanage. That's where they went.'

'Just give us a second,' said Perry. He was tapping something into his phone. After a moment, he looked back up at Macleod. 'Not a lot of results. In fact, the only one I can get is a newspaper report about it. So it must be very low profile.'

'Does it say where it is, though?'

'Garve,' said Perry. 'Looks like it's in Garve.'

'Out on the Ullapool road,' said Macleod.

'One and the very same.'

'So that's the next port of call,' said Macleod. 'We head for Garve and Appleseed Orphanage.'

'Plan of attack is?' asked Kirsten.

'Well, we find out who they are, what they do. We talk to them.'

'We talk to them,' said Kirsten. 'So basically, this orphanage has taken the son of someone who possibly was killed. Beginning to get to a familiar pattern,' said Kirsten.

'How do you mean?' asked Perry.

'Gavin Isbister's wife,' said Macleod, 'got married off to someone who basically lived with her and made sure she shut up. Now you've got a child off to an orphanage.'

'Exactly,' said Kirsten.

'But the thing that it also tells us,' said Macleod, 'is somebody's got a heart despite all that they want to keep this society secret. They don't just despatch all the children and all the wives. They seem to have a way of controlling them, or at the very least, giving them a chance in life.'

'You should tell that to the Revenge group. Most of them didn't seem to get that,' said Perry.

'No, but they weren't working for them. It's people who were working for the group, their children, relatives. I think there's something in that,' said Macleod. 'I'm not sure what.'

'Well then,' said Kirsten, 'let's go to Garve and find out.'

Chapter 06

Perry pulled the car up in Garve, a small village on the Ullapool road. It had taken a good half an hour out of Inverness to get there, and he noted that the old hotcl was all boarded up. Despite that, there was a brand-new village hall. Perry wondered just what sort of community it was. He sat in the car and Macleod looked at him.

'So, we do what, just knock on the door.'

'I wouldn't do that,' said Kirsten.

'Well, we've got to find some stuff out,' said Macleod. 'We can't hang about for too long.'

'When Anna Hunt says don't hang about, she doesn't mean you charge in full throttle,' said Kirsten. 'We're not talking about being like the Light Brigade here. Instead, what we're looking for is a bit of impetus, not recklessness. I suggest we watch the building, at least for a day. See if we can work out what goes on there. See if it is an orphanage, or if it's something else.'

'Okay, so how do we do it?' asked Macleod.

'Well, why doesn't Perry drop you and me off? Find a spot to watch from,' said Kirsten.

'Alternatively, Perry can get the bus somewhere else,' said

Macleod.

'Sorry,' said Perry to his boss. 'What do you want me to do?'

'Get whatever you can on this Appleseed orphanage off the net, or anywhere else. We'll see you back here tonight.'

Perry nodded, left the car, and headed off for the train station. It was all of a couple of hundred yards away. Kirsten slipped into the front seat of the car, beside Macleod.

'You okay?' she asked.

'I just want to get going. I just want to sort it.'

'So does everyone else, but you've got to be patient.'

'You may not be aware, but although I work in the murder squad, I'm not used to seeing dead bodies floating down the canals. It's not what I'm about. Murder to us is quite shocking. But she was dispatched in cold blood. Something else entirely.'

'When you become part of the Service,' said Kirsten, 'you learn two things. One is how to bide your time. Two, how to move quickly, so quickly nobody sees it coming. Whether you're successful in the Service depends on knowing when these times are and then executing them. At the moment, this is a bide-your-time moment. We jump in too quickly, they shut ranks. We don't get what we need here. And that's the thing, remembering the goal.'

'To bring down the Forseti group,' said Macleod.

'No, not to bring them down; to identify them,' said Kirsten. 'That's our mission, is to identify them. They get brought down, excellent, but we need to identify them, especially the head honcho. We need to know who makes it tick and who keeps it working. If we know that, other options are available.'

'I want to finish it, to sort them out. I want to lock them up,' said Macleod.

'I hope you get your wish,' said Kirsten. 'But that's not the aim. The aim is to identify them, and sometimes that means not getting in their face, but watching from a distance.'

'Then I shall watch,' said Macleod.

By the time Perry returned that night, Macleod had more than his fill of watching. They'd seen a couple of children come out of the building, accompanied, and go back in. But very little else had happened.

'Did you learn anything?' Macleod asked Perry as he sat in the back seat.

'I was able to get into some records, and it turns out that they have ten children of various ages. But the orphanage roots are back in the sixties. That's when they started.'

'And they still only have ten children?' said Macleod.

'It's not an open thing. You don't just get sent here randomly. It's different to public institutions. Private. Records aren't easy to get at. I'm struggling to get the names of the children. But they get a clean bill of health. They've had a clean bill of health ever since the sixties.'

'That's unusual, isn't it?' said Kirsten.

'We have a problem with the inspection records, and we don't know the kids' names. Somebody is covering for them. I can go deeper with it,' said Perry, 'but I thought I would wait. I didn't know what I would stir up if I went looking too closely.'

'Do we need to do what we did in the last place?' asked Macleod.

'How do you mean?' asked Kirsten.

'Our Perry here is a man of the people. Why don't we get Perry talking to them? They haven't seen him about yet. What you could do with is looking a bit different though,' said Macleod.

'How do you mean?' asked Perry.

'We could do with you being a hiker, somebody making their way through, then you could ask anyone you met appropriate questions.'

'I might have something in the bag,' said Kirsten. She left the car and went into the boot before coming back inside with a bag. Inside the car, she sorted out some items of clothing and handed them to Perry.

'Disappear, come back from the station and then get talking to people from the orphanage,' said Macleod. 'We'll keep an eye to make sure you're not pestered by the locals.'

Perry disappeared and when he came back, he had long woollen socks on with trainers. He had shorts which showed rather precarious knees and Macleod couldn't help but gawk at Perry's waterproof jacket. He looked like the most unlikely hiker. But it was a perfect disguise.

Perry would be coming off the train and he wouldn't go far before getting back on. He looked like a proper tourist. Perry walked past the car, and Macleod rolled down the window.

'You know where this Appleseed Orphanage is?' said Perry to Macleod, in a rather droll American accent.

'Perfect. See you soon,' said Macleod, who rolled up the window.

Perry began walking through the village. He saw a woman hanging up her washing, and from the bottom of her driveway, gave her a shout. 'Hello,' he said. 'I'm Randy McNicol, you live here?'

'I don't often put washing up on somebody else's line,' said the woman.

'No, no, I guess you don't. I need a little bit of assistance, ma'am, if you could help me.'

The woman came over and Perry looked straight at her. 'I've

just got off the train, and I can't see the ferry.'

'The ferry? What ferry?'

'You have some islands or something, haven't you? I was going to pop out there, get the ferry for the day and come back again, but I don't see no ferry.'

'You're in Garve,' said the woman. 'You're miles from the coast and besides, the train doesn't go to the ferry. You'd have to get a bus.'

'Oh dang, darn it,' said Perry. 'You got to be kidding me. I'm going to have to go all the way back into Inverness?'

'In Inverness, get the bus in the morning,' said the woman.

'That's unreal. Well, where am I then, anyway?'

'You're in Garve,' said the woman.

'Garve? Like what? How do you spell that?'

'G-A-R-V-E,' said the woman.

'Garvey? You're in Garvey?'

'Garve,' said the woman. 'I guess you'd better go back for the train.'

'Well, I don't know. Tell me something, though. I walked past something on the way down. It's called Appleseed. We have a church called Appleseed. It's not a church, is it? We had a church of that name.'

'It's not a church; no, it's an orphanage,' said the woman. 'Been here for years. Started way back in the sixties.'

'The sixties? You mean like when the Beatles were about?'

'Yeah, got it spot on. That's when the Beatles were about,' said the woman.

'Is it like a house?'

'It's quite a big house, actually,' said the woman. 'I mean, they only have about ten or twelve kids, something like that.'

'All right. I was thinking I might have popped in, see if they were connected to the church.'

'They're not connected to the church. It's an orphanage on its own.'

'Sure, but you're talking about the sixties. The Appleseed church was going from back in the sixties, at least, if not before. So, they might have had something to do with it. I wonder what would be the best way to get a hold of them? Should I just pop in?'

'We don't tend to see much of them,' said the woman. 'I mean, it keeps itself to itself.'

'How do they do that? I mean, don't the kids come out? You'd take kids out and about, wouldn't you?'

'If they do, the minibus comes and takes them away,' said the woman. 'They don't tend to walk around the village here.'

'Really? Is there anything else about them I should know? I'm wondering, should I talk to them at all now? But if it's got the church connection?'

'I don't think it will have the church connection,' said the woman. 'I mean it. It's probably not your Appleseed, wherever that's from.'

'It's from America,' said the man. 'Quite big, though. One of these planting churches. You go and plant a church somewhere and then it grows. They got ministries here, there, and everywhere. Wonderful, wonderful what God can do sometimes, isn't it?'

'Absolutely,' said the woman, although she didn't seem to think it was that wonderful. She started to edge back towards her washing. 'You ever seen anybody from in there though, like any of the adults, not just the children?'

'Well, there seems to be a boss that comes,' said the woman. 'Rather attractive older woman—I mean in her sixties.'

'Was everything in the sixties around here?' Perry gave a hollow laugh and the woman gave one back to him.

'No,' said the woman. 'The thing is that every now and then we get this woman roll up. Older woman, but she seems to get treated like royalty. The staff come out, they welcome her, take her in. She seems to stay for a few hours and then she goes again. Happens every few weeks.'

'And you think she is something? You think she would know about the sixties? She could tell me if it is an Appleseed church?'

'I can tell you it won't be Appleseed Church. I've never seen a church or any cross or anything to do with them over there,' said the woman.

'I don't know, but sometimes they get a bit quieter when they're in places. You know, not everyone is as happy as the good old U.S.'

Perry was wondering how much he could push the accent. The thing was, if he was in America, he would probably get his cover blown because he didn't think it was a particularly good accent. He was trying to go for the deep south, but he would wander every now and again. And besides, natives to those areas would pick him out a mile off. But it was something about being in another country. Everybody assumed an accent for a foreigner. Perry was just playing into it.

'Well then, maybe I can find her. You said she was what? An attractive woman?'

'Older, in her sixties. Like I say, she's tall, she's got long black hair, and she's got sunglasses. Always sunglasses.'

'Well, that was mighty fine of you to tell me,' said Perry. 'I'm going to get on now. Maybe I'll pop back out, see it again. Shame not to get in.' Perry made his way back, towards the train station before changing inside the men's toilets and then returning to the car.

'How did it go?' asked Macleod.

'Well, I think my old American charm just reaped dividends.'

'Seriously, Perry, what happened?'

'Well,' said Perry, 'it seems that Appleseed's been there since the sixties. Doesn't mix at all. You see the kids going out in minibuses. There is a woman who comes every once in a while, long black hair wearing sunglasses. That's about it.'

Macleod turned round to Kirsten. 'I don't know how long we can keep this up. Not an awful lot to find out there, is there?'

'We don't want to blow it,' she said to Macleod.

'Well, I don't know about you, but I'm tired,' said Macleod. 'Why don't you take watch, Kirsten? I can take it after you. I'm going to phone the others, see if anything else is going on today.'

Chapter 07

'What's this call about?' asked Clarissa.

'A request came in to look at some stolen items. They think they're antiques,' said Patterson. 'I said we'd get over.'

'Do they know their antiques?' asked Clarissa.

'When do they ever know if they're antiques? That's why they want us to look at them,' said Patterson.

'I don't like this. I don't like this when there are plenty of other things going on, things we could get stuck into and to help.'

'This is the job,' said Patterson. 'You're just hyped up because you're not out in all those exciting exploits anymore. Me? I'm happy doing the job. This is what we signed up for.'

'Things aren't sorted yet,' said Clarissa. 'When they're not sorted, well, you don't go off doing other things.'

'The boss has got it in hand. He knows what he's doing. Let him do it.'

'It'll not be the first time he's got it wrong,' said Clarissa. 'I had to sort him out before. I had to rescue him.'

'I think everyone knows that.'

'What are you saying?'

'I'm just saying that I think everyone is well aware of what you've done. Now, can we get out the door?'

'I'll take my car,' said Clarissa.

'When do we not?'

'Well, we haven't had it for a while, doing these other jobs.'

'Well, I'm beginning to like them again,' said Patterson.

Clarissa threw him a look, before standing up from behind her desk, and grabbing her tartan shawl, flinging it around her. She barked at Patterson to make a move, and the pair of them walked down to the small green car in the car park behind the station.

'How far away is it?' asked Clarissa. 'Do you have directions?'

'You said you were driving. I thought you were going to get the directions,' said Patterson.

'I'm doing the executive function of driving the car,' said Clarissa. 'You need to be looking after the map details. Now let's go.'

Patterson gave a deep sigh, but he knew it was coming and he already had a route done up on the maps in front of him.

'Ten minutes,' said Patterson. 'Five the way you drive.'

'There's no need for that.'

The day was a bright one, and although there was hint of a possible shower in the air, there was little breeze. Clarissa drove with the top down and the wind passing through her hair. Because they were going through Inverness, she didn't have time to really open up with the little ground sports car.

She felt good with the air blowing past her face. It's what she enjoyed. Out and about. And maybe Patterson had a point. Maybe it was good getting back to the old job. Not the things they'd been involved in recently. There'd been a few situations that, well, she didn't want to think about them. But what was driving her on was Frank. They'd tried to kill Frank. People couldn't be allowed to do that, and they were still out there.

'Is this it?' Clarissa said, pulling the sports car up outside a small warehouse.

'Yes, they found the stash in the back, apparently.'

Clarissa stepped out of her car and walked over to the front door where she saw a constable. She went to march past him.

'You're not showing ID,' said the constable.

'It's DI Urquhart,' said Clarissa and went to walk past him.

'I'm sorry,' he said. 'I don't know you.'

Clarissa turned to look at Patterson. He almost burst out laughing but reached inside his pocket. He pulled out his warrant card.

'Detective Constable Eric Patterson, this is DI Clarissa Urquhart. You're not long at the station.'

'Transferred up two days ago,' said the man.

'That explains a lot. Most people know DI Urquhart.'

'It's the stylish attire,' said Clarissa, and marched past the bewildered constable.

Patterson shook his head and told the young constable not to worry about it.

Once inside, Clarissa looked over towards the items they had been called about. They seemed to be stashed in a corner, although there was a column close by.

'We got anyone in charge?' asked Clarissa.

'DI Urquhart,' said a man waving from the corner. He was wearing a police uniform with sergeant stripes and came over to shake her hand. 'John,' she said. 'What have you got for me?'

'Sorry to bring you out, Clarissa, but I can't tell a trap from the real thing. Have a look over there. See if this is worth anything for me, will you?'

'Of course. How did you find out about it?'

'Confidential phone call. That's the thing. We don't get that many confidential phone calls reporting in about jewellery and other items. Then we came in and they're all stashed like this.'

'Has anyone touched them?' asked Clarissa.

'Not really. We had a little hoke about just to see if there was anything hidden away within them, but it just looks like, well . . .'

Clarissa looked at him. Apparently, the man was trying not to say what he thought, but instead was trying to say what he thought she would like him to say.

'Like what?' said Clarissa.

'Paraphernalia?'

'I'm not sure the DI would appreciate that, Sarge,' said Patterson, but he had a big smile on his face.

'The DI would not,' said Clarissa. 'I'll see if there are items of note, and not just general paraphernalia.'

Clarissa began to hoke through the items before her and picked up a couple of necklaces. There were somewhat neat stones within it. She took it over to one side and looked around for a table.

'Anywhere I can set anything down?' asked Clarissa.

'Of course,' said the sergeant. He turned and waved his hand at one constable. The man disappeared into another room before coming in with a small table.

'It's all we can find,' said the constable.

'It's fine,' said Clarissa, and placed the necklaces down on it.

'I'm just wondering if you would want to look at that column over there,' said a voice.

Clarissa looked around and saw a police constable standing

in front of her.

'I'm sorry,' she said.

'Just wanted to know if you wanted to look at the column. It's got some ornate stonework.'

'Don't want to look at the stonework. These necklaces are excellent,' she said. She turned back to look at them, then turned round to show them to the constable. But he was gone. 'I don't know,' she said to herself. 'People these days are too quick to want things that they want, not listen to people that know.' She continued to look at the jewellery for a few minutes, before turning and looking for her colleague. 'Pats,' she said. 'Come over here. Tell me what you make of this stuff.'

Patterson wandered over, drawn away from talking to one of the constables. He peered at the items.

'Well, worth quite a bit, I would have thought. Especially with those stones.'

'Look at the work on the necklace, though,' said Clarissa. 'That's sharp. That's really good. It's worth more than a bit. It makes little sense to me. Why would you leave these here? In amongst all this nonsense. Rubbish like this.'

'Rubbish,' said Patterson. 'Some of the other items there, I would say, are worth a bit too.'

'Good, but not compared to stuff like this. Pats, you really need to work out what's really important and what isn't.'

'Of course,' said Patterson. He picked up the necklace and took another look at it. 'It is indeed excellent. I'm just going to pop outside. Apparently, the guy on the door was one of the first here. I just want to see if he saw anything.'

'You do that,' said Clarissa. 'This has probably been stashed for a while though.'

Clarissa continued to look at the necklaces, and then turned to look for where everyone else was. The sergeant had left the room, and she spotted a constable walking in.

'Oh,' he said. 'Inspector. Have you had a chance to look at the column yet?'

'The column. Why would I look at the column? The column's worth nothing compared to this lot. It doesn't even look genuine to me.'

'That's strange. We've got a match for it.'

'A match for it. How do you mean?' asked Clarissa.

'Apparently, it may have come from a Greco-Roman temple. Looks like it's been cut out.'

Greco-Roman temples were not Clarissa's strong point. Maybe the man was right.

'How old would you think it is?' asked the constable.

'I'd need to take a detailed look at it and probably do a bit of research. It's not really my forte. We don't have lots of columns lying around. Not up here in the north of Scotland. I tend to deal with more with jewellery, items like that, or knives. But it could be worth something if that's what it is,' said Clarissa. 'Hard to move it too. Can't understand why it's here. Don't understand why the rest of it's here. I'm just going to talk to Pats here,' said Clarissa, seeing Patterson walk in the door. 'Then I'll take a look at it for you, okay?'

'Thank you, Inspector. I'll just be outside,' said the Constable.

The Constable departed, watched by Patterson, before Clarissa waved him over.

'Greco-Roman, apparently, according to that Constable. Said they've got a match for the column, so I'm going to take a quick look at it. You know anything about Greco-Roman columns?'

'Not really,' said Patterson. 'I haven't really done anything on them. Masonry, stonework, you haven't given me anything to learn on that.'

'No, because it's usually quite dull,' said Clarissa. 'However, it is what it is, and I'd better go look.'

The sergeant walked in as Clarissa walked past Patterson and headed off towards the column.

'How's the Inspector getting on?' asked the sergeant to Patterson.

'You've definitely got some items here. She'll fill you in. She's just checking out that column. Apparently you've got a match for it.'

'We've got a what?' said the sergeant.

'You've got a match for it. One of your constables said you've matched it. Graco Roman.'

'Which constable? I know nothing about this.'

'The tall brown-haired constable,' said Patterson. 'Just gone out. Not a moment or two ago.'

'I haven't got anybody tall and brown here,' said the sergeant. 'You sure you got that right?'

'They've literally just left. Tall and brown-haired.'

'Not with me today,' said the sergeant.

'Just hold it there a minute,' said Patterson. He cut through the door that the constable had gone out, but couldn't see him in the next room. The door, however, to the outside was swinging, and Patterson ran over to it. When he opened it, he could see the constable walking over towards a plain car. He was taking something out in his hand. It looked like it had a switch.

Something dawned on Patterson—something unpleasant. At that moment, his mind was being challenged with two things. What was the device the constable pulled out in his hand? And why had they been so focused on getting Clarissa to go to that column? He could see the constable turn and look into the warehouse through a large window. He would have direct line of sight to Clarissa. Patterson turned on his heel. He ran to the door, threw it open, ran through the small room and burst in past the sergeant to see Clarissa standing over the column beside the window.

'Get out of the way.'

'Pats? What?'

Patterson hadn't stopped. He hit Clarissa at full bore, as hard as he could. She spun round, hit the ground, and started rolling away. Patterson stopped, turned, began to run himself, but then an almighty sound filled his ears. He felt himself lift.

The sergeant across the room was far enough away that the explosion from the column didn't knock him off his feet. He did, however, raise his hands to protect himself. They didn't prevent him from seeing Patterson be lifted off his feet into the window, smashing it, and then falling outside.

On the floor, Clarissa could feel her ears ringing, but she couldn't hear properly, and was dazed. She staggered up onto her feet, fighting with everything she had to keep moving. She started waving at the sergeant, who was yelling at her, but she couldn't hear anything. Struggling, she tottered across, past the now-exploded column, and her feet crunched on the glass of the window.

There wasn't that much inside, most of it having been blown outside, but some had managed to fall down in the middle of that melee. As she got to the window, she looked outside and saw the motionless Patterson on the floor. There was blood running from his face. She turned, running as hard as she could, out of the room.

She staggered, ears not recovered. Beating her to him was the sergeant.

'Ambulance,' screamed Clarissa. 'Ambulance.' The sergeant was already on the radio and he looked at her, for she didn't know how loud she was shouting. Her ears still rang from the noise of the explosion. She recognised the constable from the front door, running over, saw the sergeant bark instructions at him, but could not hear a word that was said. She reached forward, looking to do CPR, but the sergeant pushed her back.

He was saying something, but she couldn't fathom what he was saying. The sergeant seemed to get the message when Clarissa put her hands to her ears, pointing; he spoke right in front of her face, slowly, and Clarissa mouthed the words that he said to her. He's breathing.

She could feel some tears coming to her eyes. She should get after whoever did this. However it happened. But who did it? How? What did Pats know? He had shoved her clear. Clarissa fell backwards onto her backside. She could feel herself beginning to shake. She was in shock.

'But he's breathing,' she said. 'He's breathing.'

Chapter 08

It was dark, well past midnight, and Macleod watched around him as he walked along the street. He was making for a small concrete bus shelter, and as he got close, he carefully peered around the corner into the dark. Seeing no one, he stepped inside and sat down on the small plastic run of a bench that had been put in a few years previously. He sat there and then heard the rain fall.

In the distance, he heard footsteps coming. They were clipping along the pavement. But out here, it would be unusual to have anyone coming. The buses had long since stopped running past this spot, and he thought it must be his contact. He sat waiting, and then saw, in the shadows, a woman step in. She was tall, with her hair pulled back into a ponytail, but she wasn't wearing a leather jacket. Instead it was a long coat, and once inside she turned to smile. But it was forced.

'What's up?' asked Macleod.

'You heard about the explosion?'

'I saw on the news there was an explosion in a warehouse.'

'Yes,' said Hope, now moving over to sit beside Macleod. 'Clarissa and Patterson were called out to identify some arts materials. When they got there, apparently there was a rogue constable who got Clarissa to go close to one item. Patterson clocked it, pushed her out of the way, but a bomb exploded from the item she was looking at. Threw Patterson out a window.'

Macleod went cold. 'How is he?'

'He's badly cut. Severe. A laceration down to the leg. He's going to be out of action for a few weeks. Hospital for a week or two, probably. He's very lucky. So is Clarissa.'

'Is she okay?'

'She escaped, practically uninjured. Sore ears from the explosion but she's apoplectic. She's raging at me. Wants in with you, wants to sort this. She wants blood. That's Frank they've gone after. Now Patterson. They couldn't have hit her harder. Unless they took you.'

Macleod pondered for a moment, then said, 'Tell Clarissa I need her to stay put and do her job. I need her to do that while I investigate. They need to see that we're not going after them.'

'Seoras,' said Hope, quietly but firmly, 'they don't give two hoots. They're coming for us, anyway.'

'We're looking into an orphanage. We're making progress.'

'And you need to make progress a heck of a lot quicker,' said Hope. 'I don't feel safe, Seoras. Do you get me? I don't feel safe. They're targeting us. They're coming for us. I've got a little one to look after. Do you get that?'

Macleod looked at her, and she thought he was about to cry. 'That's why I'm doing this,' he said. 'I need to get them off our back. I need to put an end to this.'

'Well, you need to do it quicker. I don't feel safe,' she said. 'Neither do any of the teams. You need to end this quickly.'

'Does John know about this?' said Macleod.

'Well, he can tell how worried I am. I'm afraid it's difficult to throw a stone face up to him. He knows I'm fretting about this one. I've told him that people are watching him as well. That he's being looked after. But after what happened with Tanya, the team doesn't have the same sort of confidence in Anna's people that we used to.'

'We're looking into an orphanage,' said Macleod. 'We think we've got a serious link. There are people in that orphanage who are the children or descendants of people the Forseti group has killed or of members they let go. So we know that there are kids being looked after and that they may have connections with people the Forseti group has dealt with. We're trying to establish what they are.'

'And how long do you wait? How long until we get this sorted? Are we just to wander around back at the station? You've pulled Jane out. You've put Tanya away. The rest of us are still there in the firing line. And quite frankly, it's not pleasant.'

'I'm going as quick as I can,' said Macleod. 'We have to, well . . . we have to go as slow as possible, not open ourselves up to them. If they see us coming and they close this loop, we may have nowhere else to go.'

'If we're too slow, we might have nobody left,' said Hope. 'I need you to go quicker. I need you to sort this out at speed,' said Hope. 'I'm not just raising a concern. I'm worried, fearful.'

'Fearful,' said Macleod. 'There's never something I thought of you being fearful.'

She took his hands, pulled her pregnancy jeans forward, placing his hands on her belly. He could hear the sound of the rain outside. But then he felt a little kick. She took his hand back out.

'I am fearful for my child. You have no idea what this does

to us women. You have no idea of how it changes me. At the moment, if anyone comes for me, I will kill them because of this little one,' said Hope. 'That dogged detective, that by the book detective, would throw it all out the window for this one. Go quicker!'

'I will,' said Macleod. She got up, as did Macleod, but before she went, she turned and she hugged him tight.

'Take care, Seoras,' said Hope. 'I know you're going to go as hard as you can. This isn't normal. This is beyond what we were trained for, what we ever wanted to get into.'

'And that's why I've got to get everybody out of it,' said Macleod. 'Stay safe. Look after the little one.'

He watched her disappear from the shelter and then walked off in the opposite direction. He made his way into a small flat, a safe house of Kirsten's. Perry was watching the orphanage in the car while Kirsten was home to sleep. As Macleod entered the flat, however, she was sitting on a sofa waiting for him.

'Explosion. Warehouse. Police officer injured.'

'Hope just told me. It's Patterson. A bomb blew him out a window. He saved Clarissa's life, and he's going to be in hospital for a couple of weeks.'

'They're going to come for us,' said Kirsten. 'They're going to come for you all; they're not buying your back to normal work.'

'No, but it has to be done,' said Macleod, 'just so they don't see us coming for them.'

'As long as everyone's aware, it's hard to keep them safe over a long period of time.'

'I'm aware of that,' said Macleod. 'On that note, the orphanage—let's go in tonight.'

'What?' said Kirsten.

'Let's go in tonight. We need to know the detail of who's in there and what goes on. Let's get in there.'

'We can't rush,' said Kirsten.

'We can't hold back. It's Patterson today. Do they go at somebody again tomorrow? The day after? The day after that?' said Macleod. 'I may not have a team left next time. We have a lead so we go in. We find out what we need to know. The only thing that's going to stop me is you telling me you're not prepared to go in yet. That you need more time to scope the place.'

'I can get in,' said Kirsten. 'If you get caught though, or if you disturb staff—'

'I know,' said Macleod.

Kirsten nodded. 'Watch, hour and a half to prep, get in, get out.' She seemed to think about something. 'You're coming in with me,' she said suddenly.

'What?' said Macleod. 'I don't do the sneaking about thing.'

'You do tonight. If you want to go in now, we've got to get in and out in enough time. We've also got to search the place. I'm good, but I also could get caught up. No, I want you in with me. We want to double up on the brain power, don't want to miss something.'

'You think you can get me in and out?'

'It's an orphanage, Seoras. They're not going to have tremendous security because it's an orphanage. If they had got tremendous security over the years, it would bring in plenty of attention. This is the thing. This place is running on the quiet. No drama, no nothing and that's the way to hide something. Hide it so well that nobody ever bothered about it. Everybody just thinks it's a boring old orphanage. You're coming with me.'

It was an hour and a half later when Kirsten crept into the car Perry was sitting in. He hadn't seen her or heard her until the door opened. But he was getting used to that. She told him the plan and to keep watching and just to know that if they had to scarper, they might jump into the car and need to go. Perry stopped her before she went.

'What?' said Kirsten.

'There's a guy pulled up in a security guard's outfit. He's gone in, but he hasn't come out. I haven't seen him walk around the building once, but you don't turn up in a security guard's outfit unless you're going to be doing some patrolling or watching of some sort.'

'Thank you,' said Kirsten. She closed the car door, and the next thing Perry saw were two shadows close to the orphanage.

Macleod was dressed in black. He'd never really worn black Lycra around his legs and thought they looked a bit spindly. The t-shirt he was wearing, along with the black fleece, felt bizarre. He was out of place. This wasn't him. And the black beanie on his head was just the icing on the cake.

'No words from here,' said Kirsten. She took Macleod round the rear of the orphanage, going to a back door, whose lock she picked. She could see there was no alarm. With the door open, she let Macleod in and closed it behind her.

Quietly, she stole across what looked like a storage room, opening the door carefully. She peered out and then quickly came back. Then she peered again, before opening the door and pulling Macleod through.

They wandered down a corridor before Kirsten saw a sign that said, 'Office.' Opening the door, she could see several desks inside, and computers. Pulling Macleod over to a filing cabinet, she used her lock-picking tools to open it, and then pointed at it for Macleod to go through. She took out a device with a USB connection and plugged it into the computer.

Having done that, she made her way to the door and checked outside. Ten minutes later, she grabbed Macleod, pulling him down under the desk. The door of the room opened. A light came on, and Macleod almost went into a panic.

Kirsten held him by the shoulders and looked into his eyes. She mouthed, 'Follow me.' There were four desks in the office, and Kirsten led Macleod in a merry dance around and underneath them all. While the guard walked around, Macleod had re-closed the filing cabinet, but Kirsten was letting the computer device continue.

The guard was only in the room for five minutes then he switched the light off and left again. Kirsten pulled Macleod back out, pointed at the filing cabinet as she went to the door. Macleod spent the next while going through the files, and using his phone, he took photographs of the names of every child in the orphanage.

He also scanned around and saw the calendar on the wall. He noted the date for the next day. Angel was visiting. It was written on the wall as Angel. No name, just Angel.

When Kirsten re-entered the room, she grabbed the computer device and pocketed it. Looking around, she made sure everything was locked back up before grabbing Macleod. She led him on a dance behind the security guard this time before they got out of the building.

She got into the car beside Perry to advise him they were out again and she would relieve him at daylight. Perry simply nodded, and Kirsten stole off into the dark to collect Macleod and head back to the safe house.

'Angel comes tomorrow,' said Macleod. 'We need to follow

her. We need to.'

'We do,' said Kirsten. 'We get some sleep now, a couple of hours, then we work on the names. Perry can help with that when he comes back. But we've got to be fresh for tomorrow. We've got to be ready to go. This might be the only chance we get to follow her. If Angel's the bigwig, it might lead us on to more. Be prepared to call Anna in.'

Macleod smiled, but he was ready for his bed. And he was more than ready to remove the black getup he was in. Anna Hunt had always told him he wouldn't be any good as a spy. It wouldn't have suited him. And he was really beginning to believe her now.

Chapter 09

'Is this the place?' asked Emmett as Sabine turned the car along the driveway up to a small port-a-cabin.

'This is the quarry.'

They were just outside Inverness at a quarry mentioned in a cold case they were looking into. The quarry had been excavated many years ago and was only within the last year reopened for more blasting. Previously, several bodies had been found in it, and the case had never been solved. Emmett was looking into it, although he was dubious about whether they would get any further.

That was the trouble with a lot of the cold cases. You started into them, and you didn't solve them because there was no more information. There was nothing new coming to light. They'd already crossed off plenty of cases from the list of possibles to look into, because there was nothing else to go on, nothing further. It was one part of cold cases that never really was understood generally; that for every one you brought home, another four or five stayed cold. It didn't bother Emmett. You could only do what you could do. If they'd got away back then, mostly they'd get away with it now.

This particular case had 'will remain unsolved' written all

over it, but Emmett had decided to go through the motions, and the first motion was to see where the bodies had been discovered. There wasn't any more forensic evidence to pick up. After all, the blasting had now continued at the quarry. Maybe the look of the quarry had changed, but Emmett always liked to go to the site where the bodies were found to get in his head what it looked like. You had to feel the case as much as go through the detail.

He wasn't sure if Sabine felt exactly the same, and she never said that. She followed where he went. He was impressed at how easily she took his ideas and instruction, given that only recently he'd had to follow her lead on the Arts team.

Getting out of the car, Emmett breathed in deeply. He looked around him.

'What's up?' said Sabine.

'Patterson. I'm just thinking about what happened to Patterson. We need to be careful.'

'Macleod said that.'

'I know what Macleod said. But Sabine, we need to really be careful. What happened to Patterson, it's quite an elaborate set-up infiltrating into our colleagues. I need to make sure this guy is who he says he is.'

'It's a quarry. Quite tough to have somebody walk into the middle of a quarry. They're all going to know each other, aren't they?'

'You would think that,' said Emmett, 'but we had somebody pose as a constable to pass information on. He wasn't spotted by Clarissa or Patterson. We need to be on our guard.'

'How are you feeling about it all at the moment?' asked Sabine.

'What do you mean, "feel about it?"'

'Well. We've had family shot at, Frank. We've had Paterson now attacked. Babies stolen in the past, though that was the other side. We've been shot at. That was this side. We've had a lot, and I could go on. There's been a lot.'

'I agree it needs done. It needs sorted. These people need stopped. It's not our job though. The Service should do this.'

'I heard they were compromised.'

'Doesn't matter. They need to get on top of it. We're out of our depth,' said Emmett bluntly.

'You think Macleod's not going to get it done?'

'He'll get something done,' said Emmett. 'But he's not like the people in the Service. Kirsten, you see her, and a lot of the team act like she's one of us. She's not. She's a killer. She will get rid of people. Maybe justifiably—with good reason. But that's not Macleod. That's not Hope. That's not you and it's not me. We're police officers. We trust the law courts. At the moment, this feeling of people coming for us? It's not normal. Come on,' he said. 'Talking about it only makes it feel worse. We need to stay rational.'

Emmett approached the port-a-cabin, knocked on the door, and stepped inside. A chunky man sat behind the desk and looked up at him.

'Hello, I'm DI Emmett Grump. This is DS Sabine Ferguson. We did phone ahead.'

'Ah, so you did.' The man had a Norwegian accent, but he was also speaking in a way that gave away he'd been speaking English for some time.

'You've been over on our side of the world for a bit,' said Sabine. 'Ireland?'

'Just outside Belfast for a while. Just outside Belfast, so I was.'

Sabine smiled. 'Well, it clearly stuck to you.'

Emmett looked at the two of them, a little amused, but then said, 'Do you mind if we look at the quarry?'

'Not at all. Just let me go out and call the guys off for a bit. They're due their break anyway. So we'll get it clear, and then we can go down, and I'll show you where they found the bones that time. That's what you're wanting, isn't it? I checked today in the records and can tell you exactly where it was, though. I'm not sure it's going to look the same.'

'Well, I didn't expect it to,' said Emmett. Sabine was holding a small manila envelope. Inside were photographs taken at the time of the discovery of the bodies, and Emmett was hoping to compare them.

'If you'd just have a seat for a moment,' said the man. He stepped outside and got onto a radio. Emmett kept the door open, watching him.

'What's the matter?' said Sabine, quietly.

'I'm just making sure he is who he is,' said Emmett. 'Just being careful.'

Emmett continued to watch the man as he spoke orders into his radio. But he also seemed to be agitated and began picking up binoculars to look towards the quarry.

'Everything okay?' asked Emmett.

'We've had a few intruders popping round. Happened since yesterday when you got a hold of us. Don't know what it is. It's a quarry. Why would anybody want to look at a quarry?'

'Intruders? Kids?' asked Emmett.

'Older than kids. Been a couple, though. All fairly young.'

'Had any trouble from them?' asked Emmett.

'No, they've just been skirting around. I haven't seen anything happen because of it. Haven't noted anything.'

A voice spoke from his radio and the man turned back towards Emmett and Sabine.

'That's the boys clear. We can enter the quarry now. Come with me,' he said. Emmett and Sabine walked down into the quarry, where it took a good five minutes to walk across it and get to the site which Emmett thought he recognised. Up to the right-hand side was exactly like the photographs with the quarry cut out. There were trees beyond it, and yes, they were slightly bigger now than they had been, but it looked so familiar.

'That side hasn't been touched. We haven't gone that way. The quarry's opened out more to this side. At the moment, this pile of loose stone is where we've been digging out and now we're moving slightly more to the left. You have to watch that one. It's quite dangerous. When we blast, everybody gets out of the way just in case you get a knock-on effect,' said the foreman. 'But it's quarrying. It is dangerous. That's why you're careful when you blast.'

'So their bodies were found here back in the day,' said Emmett, turning to Sabine to ask for the manila envelope. Taking the photographs out, he stood with her, looking around and then grabbing the foreman to ask certain questions. 'How did this work? Where has the quarry been cut since? On the day when they found it, what were the locations of the bodies? How were they turned?'

The foreman knew a lot of detail, but he said it was all from the records, because he hadn't been here at the time. In fact, he'd been a young lad. Emmett looked left and right. He wasn't sure that he was really learning anything. Why down in the quarry? Why had they dumped them here? It was gangland related. He was sure of it, though it was never proved.

The foreman's radio crackled into life. He stepped aside for a moment, then came back.

'You're welcome to stay,' he said, 'but don't go anywhere else. Just work from here. There's a phone call I have to take, apparently, back up at the office.'

'You're okay with us here?'

'They can't go back in to start again until I give the go-ahead. You're fine.'

'Thank you,' said Emmett. He continued with Sabine, looking at the site, while the foreman disappeared back off towards his hut. Once he'd disappeared out of sight, Emmett continued to focus on the ground.

'Where do you think they came down?' he said to Sabine. 'Coming in at night, they would have left tire tracks, surely. They would have left something. Would they carry them in by foot?' he wondered aloud.

Before Sabine could answer, several minor explosions shook the ground. Emmett turned in shock to look at the rather large slag pile which was now on the move. Stones were tumbling down towards them. He felt Sabine grab his arm.

'Run! Bloody run,' she said. He took off as hard as he could, Sabine dragging him most of the way. From behind, rocks tumbled. A couple flew past them. The pile had collapsed, charging down the hill.

He didn't look round. Instead, with Sabine holding on to one of his hands, Emmet ran as hard as he could. She was quicker, and he was slowing her down, but she wouldn't let go of him. Dust flew past them, choking them, but together they kept running, until eventually they hit the far side of the quarry. They ran up, climbed slightly, but the sound behind them was stopping. Dust was still in the air, blowing here and there and everywhere.

'Are you okay?' asked Sabine.

'I'm good,' said Emmet.

'I'm going to see who did this,' said Sabine. She took off into the dust cloud. Emmett went to go after her, but he couldn't see where she was. He waited for he wouldn't keep up with her, anyway. As the dust pile settled, he saw Sabine at the top of the quarry, running hard.

From her position, Sabine could see a road in the distance. It wasn't far away and there was a figure heading towards it. She bolted but she was several hundred yards behind. A blue hatchback pulled up on the road. Before she got anywhere near it, she could see the figure exiting vegetation they were running through and jump into the car. It drove off.

Sabine called it in on her mobile phone asking if there were any units nearby, putting out a request to spot the car. In truth, they were looking for a blue hatchback. There was no known number plate. If they knew the road by now, it could be anywhere. Would they even be dust covered like she was?

She turned and walked back, her hair grey, sticky and powdered. When she got back to the quarry, Emmett was standing beside the foreman.

'Got into a car. I saw them run off. A man. Didn't get close enough for a detailed description. Blue car. Called it in.' Sabine was still out of breath from her efforts.

'Good. Our friend here says that there was no phone call when he got up there.'

'I thought it was one of the team on the radio. You heard the radio, its quality isn't that good. Somebody imitated a voice. Obviously wanted me out of the way. I don't understand how they got explosives planted, though.'

'You say there's been people annoying you the last little while, but they haven't done anything?' suggested Emmett.

'Legging it round the top. Down into the quarry around. Idiots. Of course, you have to make sure the place is clear. You have to make sure they've gone away.'

'They've probably distracted you while somebody else has come in and planted things. That's why they were able to set off the explosion,' said Emmett.

'At least you're okay.'

'Yes,' said Emmett. 'That is good.' He stepped to one side with Sabine. 'Kind of a rush job. Yesterday, then today. Somebody wants us out of the way and quick.'

'They must be really worried about us. They must think we can get close.'

'Either that or they want to nip us in the bud before we get anywhere,' said Emmett. 'Anyway, there's nothing here for our case.'

'No,' said Sabine. 'Except for our photographs. They're underneath that pile in there.'

Emmett looked at the scree that had tumbled down. The rocks were piled high and deep in it were photographs from the case. At least they were only copies.

'Let's head back to the station and get a shower. I've had enough of being in people's sights for the day.'

'I don't think that's going to change quickly,' said Sabine. She reached over and grabbed his hand. 'But we're still here.' He squeezed her hand back. *He's never done that before*, thought Sabine. *Never showed emotion like that.* As much as she was worried, fearful of the situation they were in, a different emotion ran through her. She wondered if it was running through him.

Chapter 10

'Seoras, are you okay?'

'A little tired,' said Macleod. 'But I'm okay. Why are you calling, Hope?'

'We've had another attack, so I thought it was worth burning one of the SIM cards to tell you. Everything's getting ramped up.'

'What happened?' asked Macleod.

'Emmett and Sabine were attacked in a quarry. Somebody blew charges, tried to put them under a slag heap collapse.'

'Are they okay?'

'They outran it. Apparently, it wasn't an efficient way of doing it, according to Emmett. He felt it was rushed. Are you getting anywhere?' asked Hope.

'Well, we've been looking into the names of the children. Perry reckons each child is a descendant of someone murdered by the Forseti group. Could be from within the group or people on the outside.'

'That's a bit strange, isn't it?'

'It's very strange,' said Macleod. 'There's a heart at the centre of this group. There's somebody that cares. This is where we have to think about the people we're dealing with.'

'In what way?' asked Hope.

'We think of them as all being people who see black and white, what's right and wrong. Therefore they're eliminating people who step too far, people who are threatening the group, people who are doing wrong in their life. It's a strange way to think, a very cultish viewpoint. But there's also a black and white line of thinking that says the children of these people did nothing wrong. So some of them have been looked after, and very well.'

'There's nobody to look after them, so we take them in as orphans.'

'That's it! Some children of the victims clearly had other people to look after them, and that's caused a bite-back, as the children gathered together and attacked the Forseti group. That's the Revenge group, but they've also taken in the children of people from within the Forseti group, we reckon, who have been killed by Forseti to protect itself, or who have killed themselves in the group's name.'

'And they set up an orphanage,' said Hope.

'Exactly,' said Macleod. 'There's a heartbeat in there that's not wholly evil. And it's got to be strong enough, high enough up to have wanted it. You can't do this, turn round and say, "Let's have an orphanage," without real influence. It's a link through to the top for us.'

'And they've done it well?' asked Hope.

'They've done it brilliantly. It's so on the quiet. Incredibly on the quiet. Simon Jolly was taken into it. That's how we tracked it. But Edderton Transport, which his father Leo Jolly ran, is never given a thought by anyone. We've been very lucky. Anna dug out a heck of a link there that we've exploited. We also know that someone called Angel is coming. This, we think, is the link into the orphanage, the big link, the person who runs this.'

'But if they set the orphanage up, they'd be really old, wouldn't they?'

'If it's them or maybe it's their prodigy, their child, whoever. The Forseti group has been running for a time, a good long time. So, maybe the orphanage is under the control of a line of people. I don't know,' said Macleod. 'All I know is that Angel is coming today and we're going to find her and follow her. Or him. Whoever it is. I just say her because you rarely call a man Angel.'

'Well, take care of yourself,' said Hope.

'No, you do it,' said Macleod. 'Have a think about how you can protect yourself more.'

'You don't think I've been doing that?'

'Think about what protection you can wear in daily life. Things as you go about the job.'

'Okay,' said Hope. 'But you move quick. We need to know what's going on, need to get through this and stop them. We're depending on you.'

'Thanks,' said Macleod. 'I didn't feel there was enough pressure.'

'Sorry,' said Hope. 'I'm just kind of on the edge.'

Macleod closed down the call and looked out of the car. Sitting beside him was Kirsten. Perry had gone to get some sleep, but now Macleod could see a car pulling up outside the orphanage.

'Looks like the right one,' said Kirsten. 'Get Perry.'

Macleod called Perry. He was asleep in a car a short distance away. As he made the call, he watched the new arrival, and a rather elegant, tall woman had the car door opened for her.

The driver wasn't quite dressed as a chauffeur, but he was in a smart suit and escorted her up to the orphanage door.

It was opened by someone from the orphanage, who welcomed the woman before allowing her to step inside. The driver made his way back to the car. Macleod and Kirsten watched as the driver sat there happily. Then he got out after half an hour and walked around. He came back to the car five minutes later and lit up a cigarette inside it. But half an hour after that, he went on another walk.

'That's the one,' said Kirsten. 'He's doing half-hourly checks. When he's out on those, that's when we bring Perry in.'

Macleod placed another call to Perry, who said he was ready to go. Macleod told him to be careful, for Perry had formulated a plan. Despite not being sure what they would glean from it, Macleod hoped Perry could find out some sort of nugget of information to break open the group. If it came to nothing, however, they still could tail Angel when she left.

* * *

Perry stretched as he got out of the car. He looked at what he was wearing. Tall hiking socks. He had a couple of walking sticks with him along with a beanie hat, a checked shirt, and a rain jacket. Having made sure he had everything, as well as a small camera that was inside one of his pockets, Perry walked to the train station.

He approached it through some trees at the rear. As a train pulled up, he walked close to it and then acted like he'd just got off it. There were few people getting off in Garve that day, but Perry mingled with the other two and then walked through the streets. He strolled close to the orphanage, spying the driver of the car coming back towards it. Perry picked up his pace. He was planning on looking like he was out of breath. But he wasn't having to act much. As he approached the driver, he was sweating and gasped at the man.

'Oh, it's warm, isn't it? It's warm today.'

'It is,' said the driver. He went to open his door, but Perry stumbled quickly and then leaned on the door, moving himself to the inside, trapping himself between it and the car. He leant back on the car.

'Oh, my goodness. It's just, they don't tell you how far places are. They don't tell you. The water's gone. The water's gone. Do you have any water?'

'I don't have any water,' said the man.

'Does anyone have any water? Get me water. I'm just so parched. I mean,' Perry slid down a bit on the side of the car, and the man reacted, grabbing him. 'Oh, thank you. Thank you,' he said. 'That's, that's so good. Oh, I need to take a moment? When I get water . . . is there any water? I don't think I can walk anywhere. Do you know that? I don't think I can walk anywhere. You need to get me some water, sir. Sorry, I'm imposing on you. I'm really imposing on you. What are you doing here?'

'I'm waiting for my client,' said the man. 'I drive her about.'

'She's here somewhere then. Is she somewhere with water? Tell me, is there water? You could . . . you could take my bottle if you want. Here, take my bottle. Take my bottle. Get me some water, please get me water! I'll watch your car, it's okay. But you get me water, please.'

The man looked at Perry and Perry did his best to faint. He let the legs go from under him and then collapsed to the ground.

The man reached down and grabbed him. 'Water, water,' said Perry.

'I'll get you an ambulance.'

'No, no, no, I just need the water. Give me water, please.'

Perry handed over his canteen. The man picked him up and sat him on the driver's seat.

'Here,' Perry said, 'here.'

The man took the canteen and walked up towards the orphanage front door. Perry sat looking at him, his head rolling, his tongue hanging out. He heard the man discussing something at the door, and then he went inside, the orphanage door closing behind.

Perry reached inside his jacket, took out the small camera, and without turning around, began taking lots of photographs of the back seat. When he'd glanced in as he reached the car, he thought he saw correspondence on the rear seat. He photographed behind him as well, the passenger seat, over and over again, until he saw the orphanage door open.

Quickly, he placed the camera back inside his jacket. It was small enough to be held within the hand, and yet, its image quality was good. Kirsten had given it to him, and Perry felt quite the spy operating it.

The driver rushed over, placing the canteen in front of Perry, opening it and then pressing it to Perry's lips. Perry drank from it, repeatedly, and then rested, still sitting in the car. He stayed there for fifteen minutes, thanking the man profusely.

Before getting up on his sticks, he said he was feeling better because of the water. Perry advised the driver he was going to try to find a cafe or something around here. If not, he'd have to make it back to the train to head on into Inverness or somewhere else. He told the man he wasn't quite sure what he was doing.

'Maybe I got off in the wrong place.'

It was another hour and a half when Perry passed the car again, saying he'd found nowhere and he was heading to the train. The driver nodded, asked him if his canteen was full and if he needed any more assistance. But Perry made it back to the train station, disappeared through the trees once a train arrived, and got back to the other car. He changed back into jeans and a t-shirt, and sat in the car, awaiting the arrival of Macleod.

* * *

'He did well,' said Kirsten. 'Very well.'

'What time do you think she'll leave?' said Macleod.

'I wouldn't have thought she'd been here for more than a couple of hours. They did say sometimes during her visits, they did little performances or something for her, so who knows?'

The pair sat together until Kirsten noted that the driver had got up. He was opening the rear door when Kirsten told Macleod to get out. Macleod stepped out of the car and began walking away from the orphanage. Behind him, Kirsten pulled away in the car and circled round. By the time Angel had got into the car and the man was driving off, Kirsten was appearing in her car behind him in a natural fashion.

Macleod was able to stop at the end of the street and watch the departure, before walking down another couple of roads and then back round past the train station and out towards where Perry had parked the car. He got in to sit beside his colleague who looked half asleep.

'Kirsten thought you did well. Have you got anything good

from your efforts?'

'I was looking at the correspondence. I've got some good photographs of it but I'll need to get back to the safe house and get a proper study of it on the laptop. Didn't want to bring the laptop out here. A bit conspicuous sitting with a laptop.'

'That's good,' said Macleod. 'We'll see where Kirsten goes. What we'll do next, I think, is call everybody together. We need to get a team meeting. The team needs to know what's going on. We've been under fire too much lately.'

'Is everyone else all right, though?' asked Perry. 'You haven't heard anything else, have you?'

'Emmett and Sabine were attacked this morning,' said Macleod. 'We need to get on to this fast, Perry. I'm thinking we have to just go for it. Go for it, push! Don't say this to anyone else, but it could only be a matter of time before one of these attacks is successful. And successful in the sense that they kill someone.'

Macleod could see Perry's worried face.

'Tanya's safe, though, isn't she?'

'Well, Tanya's very safe,' said Macleod but Perry's face still showed that he was anxious.

'Susan will be fine. She'll be okay. Ross is there. She's not daft.'

'Patterson. Now attacking Emmett and Sabine. None of them are daft,' said Perry, in an unusual raising of his tone. 'It's on us. You know that, don't you? It's on us, to get this done. To get the pressure off everyone else.'

'Yes,' said Macleod. 'I know that. I know it's on us. Trust me, Perry. I'm feeling it every bit as much as you are.'

Chapter 11

Macleod wanted his team gathered together, but it wasn't a straightforward thing to do. He wasn't meant to be there. He was meant to be on holiday with Jane. Perry was also supposed to be recuperating, so they couldn't just stroll into the police station and hold it in Hope's office. There was also a question why everyone would be in together if they were seen within the station. And given what had happened with Patterson, Macleod wasn't convinced that there weren't moles within the station.

Also, had somebody been watching Emmett and Sabine, able to pre-empt their visit out to the quarry? So instead, he called a gathering at night on Kirsten's advice. The barn was nothing special, a simple farmer's barn stuck in a field and accessible by a couple of tracks.

What had annoyed some of his colleagues was that they wouldn't be allowed to take their car right up to the barn. This especially annoyed Clarissa. She had driven there in an unfamiliar car and parked up over a mile and a half away. She had then hiked through the dark with Ross to get to the meeting. Ross had his laptop with him, but Clarissa didn't need any of that. She was coming armed with annoyance, and what had happened to Patterson was still enraging her.

Macleod and Perry had walked in from over a mile away, and the only person who had turned up in a car had been Hope. But it had been a different one. She had also picked Susan Cunningham up on the way as added protection.

Inside the barn, Ross had moved a couple of hay bales about. There weren't many, but he'd formed a ring, and Macleod sat at what Ross had designated as the top. Perry sat beside him, quiet, but he gave a smile over to Susan when she'd entered with Hope. He'd also jumped up and assisted Hope to sit down, though Hope had told him to go away. She wasn't at that stage yet. She wasn't waddling.

'Are we all here, then?' asked Macleod.

'Well, Pat's isn't,' said Clarissa tersely.

'No, he's not,' said Macleod. 'Let's see if we can put away the anger and get on?'

Clarissa sat down, almost spitting at him.

'Perry and I, along with Kirsten, have been chasing someone called Angel. We're investigating an orphanage. An orphanage that contains orphans left behind after deaths associated with the acts of the Forseti group. Sometimes within their own order, sometimes without. A rather strange situation, and one that's existed for over sixty years.

'There's a heart beating within this Forseti group. I guess it's probably like Hitler being kind to his family. But whatever it is, it exists. A woman visits the orphanage every once in a while, taken there by a driver. However, doors are held open, and she's obviously the big cheese. This is our link into the Forseti group. We have no other. Perry,' said Macleod.

Perry stood up. 'I acquired some photographs of the rear of the car she was driving. She had left some paperwork out, not much, and nothing of importance. But it did have her name on it. She is Lady Juliet Cockburn.' Perry then took out a photograph that Kirsten had taken of the woman.

'That's Juliet Cockburn,' said Clarissa. 'She's married to Lord Alistair Cockburn. He sits in the Lord's.'

'That's right,' said Macleod. 'So we're dealing with someone who's got very high up connections. Kirsten's currently watching her. Been tailing her ever since she left the orphanage. She hasn't just gone back to her own estate. She's also been to many others. In fact, I've got a list here,' said Macleod. He walked over to Clarissa and handed it to her. 'Any of these strike you?'

Clarissa looked down at them while everyone else looked on.

'There's nothing unusual in most of these, Seoras. I wouldn't have said any of them are particularly high figures, socially. Most of them are running normal estates, trying to make a living. Some old families. Except for Malcolm Varney, of course.'

'Why him?' asked Macleod.

'He's not from an aristocratic background. He's from a business background, a millionaire businessman. He's also a widower, and he's certainly not in the circles that Lady Cockburn moves in.'

'Really?' said Macleod.

'Not at all,' said Clarissa. 'The others, she would mix with without any stain on her reputation. In fact, I think she would have mixed with them for years. The families, they intermingle. That's the stock you want your children to marry into. Malcolm Varney—absolutely not. I mean, why has Cockburn got anything to do with him? He's a bit of a blunt instrument in a lot of ways. Widower too. So why would she be visiting him? I don't know. Strange, she would go on her own.'

'But that she does,' said Macleod.

'Why don't I look into it?' asked Clarissa.

'No,' said Macleod.

'I understand this side of society, know the Cockburns. I understand the people they're mixing with. Even Varney, I understand. Why wouldn't I do it?'

'She makes a good point, Seoras,' said Hope.

'No,' said Macleod.

'Why not?' said Clarissa. 'What's wrong with me doing it? Why do you not want me involved?'

'It's not the time.'

'It most certainly is,' said Clarissa. She was on her feet and walking to the centre of the circle.

'Sit down,' said Macleod.

'No, Seoras, I won't. I'm the one who can get involved here and do the most damage.'

'Exactly,' said Macleod. 'This needs to be quiet for now. They mustn't know we're coming for them.'

'They're coming for us. We're under attack, and you're expecting us just to sit here. Just to sit here and take it. We got lucky with Pats, very lucky. If it hadn't had been for him, I'd be dead. And he just about survived. What's the next one going to be? Emmett had to run,' she said, pointing over to Emmett, who had been quiet, sitting on one of the bales of hay beside Sabine.

'We are. Actually, we have been lucky,' said Emmett. 'We were fortunate that ours was a badly planned attack.'

'And ours wasn't,' cried Clarissa. 'We need to get this done quickly. We need to get in, find who they are, take them down.'

'Take them down? I hope you mean arrest them,' said Macleod.

'I think we're beyond that, aren't we, Seoras?' said Clarissa. 'Why is Anna Hunt not involved? Because she doesn't know who they are. When she knows who they are, she can sort it.'

'We're the police here,' said Macleod. 'Don't ever forget that!'

'The police? I legged it halfway across to Heligoland. Anywhere else, police don't do that. Not that way. Not the way we were doing it. I think we left our basic police training behind.'

'Don't. It's the only thing that keeps us where we are. This group has stepped in. The Forsetis,' spat Macleod. 'They've destroyed what policing is. You obtain evidence, and then you put them away. And that's what we'll do with them. We will not become them.'

'It's the only way to beat them,' said Clarissa.

'You can walk, if that's what you think,' said Macleod. And then noticed that Hope was on her feet.

'Easy,' said Hope. 'Easy. We're a team, remember? A team. And we need each other more than ever, especially with what's going on. She's right though, Seoras. We need to sort this out quick. We might have to push in a fashion that we're not used to.'

'We're doing the best we can, but I can't rush too much,' said Macleod. 'Kirsten understands this world, understands how to go about it.'

'Kirstie's used to people dying around her, Kirstie's used to her own team not always making it.'

'You don't know that,' said Macleod.

'Kirstie's changed. Kirstie's Service,' raged Clarissa.

'You didn't know her. You don't know her,' thundered Macleod.

'Can we just take it easy?' said Hope.

'She has a point,' said Emmett, quietly. 'How does this end? You seriously think we're just going to arrest them? The time for that is long gone. When there were two groups and people with evidence, then maybe. Maybe we could have done it. But we just said that we've got a guy who sits in the Lords, possibly near the top of this. We need to know how this finishes,' said Emmett.

'No, we don't,' said Hope. 'What we need to do is to find them first. When we find them and we know who they are . . . then we can end it.'

There was silence amongst the group. Macleod spoke quietly.

'I need you all to be doing your normal jobs. Give the impression that we have stopped looking. Even if all it is, is giving the impression that we've stopped looking. Or we've called a hiatus for the moment. That we've stopped. Certainly for the present time; hopefully, they'll think we won't be continuing later. They can't think that I'm doing anything except being on holiday. Tanya away too. Your continuing your cases says that's what I'm doing.'

'I know what you're saying,' said Emmett, 'but I'm not sure it works. It's good that you've got your partner out of the way. Tanya too. Thank goodness for Perry or she'd be dead.'

'And that's what I mean,' said Clarissa. 'They're coming for us. Frank would be dead except for Anna Hunt. We'll let Anna deal with it. Let me get in, find out who these people are, and we'll hand everything over to Anna Hunt.'

'This is a police investigation. It may be undercover, it may be specialist, but I am running it and I am not about to get dictated to by Anna Hunt,' said Macleod.

'Why don't you tell that to Pats!' said Clarissa. 'See if that comforts his back. See if that helps him get better quickly. He's not with me anymore. What happens next time? I'd just die.'

'You're not coming in with us,' said Macleod. 'When I need people, I will call them.'

'Seoras is the boss,' said Hope. Her voice was deliberate, firm, and not asking for debate. 'It's his call. It's his plan. We've questioned it. He's made his decision. We need to move on, Clarissa, whether you agree with it or not.'

Macleod thought Clarissa had taken the hump with him. She sat with her arms folded underneath her shawl.

'Can I suggest,' said Hope, 'that Ross gets on to a list of Varney's businesses? If Juliet Cockburn is going to meet him, she's either having an affair with him or she's needing him for some other reason. So, let's get deep into who he is and what he's doing. That'll be a good one for Ross to do from a distance. We'll leave the close-up to Kirsten and yourself,' said Hope.

'And the rest of us just go back,' spat Clarissa.

'The rest of you just go back,' said Macleod. He adjourned the meeting, and Clarissa departed with Ross, Emmett with Sabine. But Hope remained, causing Susan to stay. Perry got the hint and took Susan outside, leaving Macleod alone with Hope.

'She has got a point,' said Hope. 'Clarissa does know the lie of the land with these people. She's sharp on them.'

'The woman is bold and reckless,' said Macleod. 'She could warn them we're coming and we'd miss them completely. This could be the last chance to get into them for who knows how long. And if we do batter our way in, they know we're still investigating. They won't stop coming after us. I need to know I've got somebody who will not go off the rails on this one. Kirsten, Perry. They're both good at that. You would be in too, except for the way you are.'

'Be careful. You're not using all the team's skills. You're going to need everyone. She's got skills. Good skills.'

'And Clarissa's got an attitude a mile wide,' said Macleod.

'And you haven't at the moment. You're not reeling from this. This is not you. You sit over the top. You're quite happy to give people a freer reign.'

'Normally my people are not the subjects of attempted murder,' said Macleod. 'Normally I have police procedure to hide bchind. I have everything in place. Not now. We are exposed. I said to you before, be very careful. Think about what measures you can take. They're coming for us, and I can see them coming for you.'

'Don't worry about me,' said Hope. 'I will look after myself. You need to focus on making sure that you are sharp in what you are doing. Don't narrow this down to become your personal vendetta, because your team is under attack.' She was pressing her finger into his chest now, and he gave her a look that let her know he was not impressed with that.

'I am not on a vendetta. We just need to get this solved and quick.'

'I have known you longer than anybody else that was here,' said Hope. 'Have seen you under pressure. I have seen you under stress, and I have never seen you handle things like this. You once told me to look at the team, to use all of the team. Do that. Listen to yourself,' said Hope. 'Take your own advice, and take care of yourself.'

She leaned forward and kissed him on the cheek. She went to go, but he stopped and hugged her.

'You take care of yourself too,' he said. 'We're all under pressure.'

Hope nodded, walked to the door where Susan joined her, disappearing off to the car. Perry came back inside, and they switched off the lights of the barn before walking out into the dark.

'You must be pretty confident,' said Perry, 'that we're not being followed or we're being watched.'

'What makes you say that?' asked Macleod.

'Well, I'm your company, and not Kirsten.'

Macleod gave a grin. 'Well, yes, I think you've got me there.'

Chapter 12

Perry had come back from the meeting and gone straight out to take over from Kirsten, allowing her some time to rest. That night, Lady Cockburn had not gone out, but had stayed in and received visitors from a couple of other landowners in the area. They were from the section of the list that Clarissa said was not a problem.

Having taken over from Kirsten, Perry sat with his flask of coffee, drinking and wondering about the meeting he'd just been at. It had been rough, to say the least, but now he had a night of sitting here doing nothing, waiting for Kirsten to come back in the morning and take over.

She would only be away for about six hours. But Macleod had insisted she'd get sleep because he didn't know how long things would go on for. Kirsten had said she didn't need sleep, but Perry had thought that would be wrong. She should sleep. She must have slept in the Service. Nobody can go too many days without it. And who knew what was coming up ahead?

He was sitting and humming a tune he hadn't heard in ages, trying to work out where it had come from, when he saw the front door of the estate house open. Somebody came out quietly and he thought he recognised her through the binoculars. It was certainly a tall, elegant woman of sorts.

She got into a car that looked rather nondescript. Perry watched the car come down the drive and leave via the front gate. As it did so, he trained his binoculars on the driver; it was Juliet Cockburn, off out on her own.

She didn't do that. Normally, she went with someone, but here she was, out and about. Perry started the car, following her at a distance, and found that she went via cross-country roads, in what was a rather bland Land Rover. Skirting the north of Inverness, he followed as she eventually made for the Falls of Shin. When she turned off the main road and took a right up the hill to the Falls, Perry wondered what the best thing was to do. He knew you couldn't get out from there, not without coming back down. So, he parked the car a little way along.

He sent a message to Kirsten, saying that the woman was at the Falls of Shin. Perry knew what the routine was. He should stay put. That's what Kirsten always said. And he expected her to give a message back to say she was on her way, any time.

Perry waited ten minutes, but still there was no response. Quietly, Perry got out of the car. He went into the boot and pulled out a black jacket, along with a black beanie. His trousers were already black, and he had boots on. Geared up, Perry locked the car and began walking towards the Falls of Shin.

She surely wouldn't be going on anywhere else, so even if she came back down and passed him, it would probably be okay. She would return to the estate. What he didn't need to do was to lose her. After all, Kirsten wouldn't be happy about that. Perry thought he was okay with doing this quiet observation. Kirsten would approve.

He tiptoed to the side of the road and then disappeared into the trees, climbing the hill to the visitor centre. He was careful, walking along through the undergrowth.

Perry couldn't see anybody as he made his way through the trees and eventually came towards the river. He took his binoculars and peered out into the dark. There were two shapes on the bridge. Perry focused in to see a man and a woman who were romantically entangled.

It looked quite passionate to Perry, but he also thought it was rather a strange place. He tried to see who the man was. Since the meeting, he'd seen a photograph of Malcolm Varney sent to the team by Clarissa. He was the right shape and size for Varney on the bridge. But Perry couldn't confirm it was him. If it wasn't, who was she seeing now and in such a way? Certainly, her husband didn't know.

Perry crept forward a little more and then froze. Off to his left was a man, standing quietly, looking around. He wasn't watching the lovers on the bridge. He was watching everywhere else. Perry crouched down and didn't move. He scanned the surrounding area, carefully now, slowly, and identified at least another two men. Again, they were not watching the scene on the bridge, but watching the undergrowth.

Kirsten had said that every time you got in trouble, one of the best things to do was freeze if they couldn't see you. Don't keep moving and show them where you are. Freeze and you decide what you're going to do. So Perry froze.

He could see guns prominently on the hips of the men. They weren't hiding them very well, and they were clearly for quick use if need be. Meanwhile, on the bridge, the couple continued with their heavy petting, oblivious to the surrounding men.

Maybe it is believed to be a romantic place, thought Perry. *The water rushing beneath you, the falls just beside you, out of the way as well.*

Perry wondered what he should do next. He knew that he'd come up to see what was going on against what Kirsten normally said. Stay in the car, observe from there. But Lady Cockburn had gone to a place where he couldn't take the car. He thought about checking his phone, but he didn't want to bring any light into the dark tableau. Hence, he wasn't sure if there was a message back from Kirsten or not. He didn't even have the vibration function on meaning he depended totally on checking the phone. But here in the dark, the light would have been so bright it might give him away.

About an hour later, the couple on the bridge stopped their embrace and their talk. Watching, Perry saw them leave and head back up towards the car park. The other men, however, didn't go up there. Instead, they started to sweep through the area, checking out the shadows and undergrowth.

Perry remained frozen, but they would come to his area soon. They would walk through here. That's the pattern they were following. They would be—

Perry felt himself disappear backwards as a hand went over his mouth and he was pulled hard. He went to struggle, but his arms were held forcibly, and he didn't have the strength to free them. The men were moving towards him and he felt himself being dragged out of the way.

Their search went past, but when it returned a couple of minutes later, his attacker pulled him away again. It took another three times of being moved out of the way before the men cleared the area and left. Only then did Perry feel the grip on him being relaxed.

He fully expected to be knocked on the head or handcuffed, but he stumbled forward when he was let go and turned to see who was behind him. He saw Kirsten and she was not happy. Even the ponytail sitting on her shoulder didn't break the anger that she was showing.

Perry went to speak, but she put her hand up in front of his mouth. She indicated he should stay there, and Kirsten disappeared for the next five minutes. Perry then saw his car driving up to the Falls of Shin car park. It was closely followed by a second car driven by Macleod. Kirsten got out of the first one, came over to Perry, but this time she wasn't silent.

'What the hell do you think you're doing?'

'I couldn't see her, so I came out to find them. I told you where I was.'

'Good job you did; otherwise, you'd probably be dead,' said Kirsten. 'You don't have the skills for this. This is what I do. It's why you contact me, and you wait. You don't go tearing off.'

'Is everybody okay?' said another voice. Kirsten turned round and saw Macleod.

'Why are you here?' she said. 'You should wait in the car, in case something's wrong and we have to get out quick. Don't follow me in. You don't assume it's all okay just because I've run round the place.'

'You told me to come up,' said Macleod.

'Yes, in the car and stay in it. To the car! Everybody!' hissed Kirsten. She marched them out to Perry's car in the car park and she sat in the passenger seat, Perry in the front driver's seat, and Macleod in the rear. She fixed the men in turn with an angry stare.

'We need to have a chat. Understand we play by my rules.

You can't just clear off to investigate like that. You can't just pitch up and think, oh, I'll stick my nose in here. The police force method doesn't work in here. These are not normal criminals. These are not people who are afraid to turn around and just kill you because you've seen something. So, you can't walk out like this. Perry, you can't. You can't do that. Do you understand me?'

'I think so now,' said Perry.

'Good, because he won't listen,' she said pointing at Macleod. 'I'm getting sick and tired of saving people's backsides. Especially as they haven't done what they're told. It's hard enough when you do what you're told. Things can still happen. But go around like this, and you invite disaster. Now, what did you see?' asked Kirsten.

'Lady Cockburn was on the bridge with a man. Looked about the right size and shape for Varney. But I didn't get a clear look at his face.'

'Well, I did,' said Kirsten. 'And it's Varney. She came out here with Varney. And they weren't having a quiet supper. That was a serious embrace. And those were his people. His guards. Not hers.'

'Something's up between the two of them,' said Macleod. 'If we think about it, is she seriously going to be having an affair with him? Is that what it's all about? If so, she's not being discreet. She's gone to his house. So, she must be going there for an alternative reason. You'd have to assume that if she was doing something on the quiet, Lord Cockburn in his position would have the capacity to find out and to know. So, assuming that, is she working on his behalf?'

'There are a lot of assumptions in there,' said Kirsten. 'We don't know what they're doing at the moment. The game plan should be to sit back and watch. You can't rush this. We nearly rushed it tonight. It nearly got messed up. If they'd have found Perry, we'd have been in trouble. We'd have been done. Gone. They'd have gone to ground. They might even have killed Cockburn and Varney off. If it's the Forseti group they're in.'

'Well, she's definitely Forseti. After all, she was tied to the orphanage,' said Perry.

'But we don't know what he is yet,' said Kirsten. 'We don't know if this is just her having a rough boy on the side.'

'Rough boy?' said Macleod.

'Well, you told me that Clarissa said he wasn't one of their type, so he's a rough boy, isn't he?'

'So, I'm a rough boy too, then,' said Macleod.

'If you like, but I don't sec you on a bridge like that,' said Kirsten.

'So you suggest that we just watch them for now? You think we should just hold back?' said Macleod.

'That's my advice. See what comes. Pick your opportunity.'

'We haven't got a lot of time,' said Macleod. 'What do you think, Perry?'

'I'm no expert when it comes to tailing and watching people,' said Perry. 'You've seen that tonight. But I don't think there is time. I'm loathe to go against what Kirsten's saying because she's the expert, but Seoras, what's the next thing to come? That's what scares me. The Forseti group has shown no signs of stepping back from us. They haven't bought the ruse of we're stepping away, leaving it all to Anna Hunt. Instead, they've come after us. Wholesale. I know what you're saying, that if we go after them too quick and they spot us, that's it— we've lost all connection. But if we don't go quick enough, we'll lose something more precious,' said Perry. 'We lose people.'

'Now's not the time to think too much about it,' said Kirsten. 'It's the middle of the night. We've had a close one but Perry's okay. We're unscathed. Let's get back, and get our tail set up again. Get a decision done in the morning.'

'Good idea,' said Macleod.

'Well, I'll take the car,' said Perry. 'Get back on to watch.'

'I'm coming with you,' said Kirsten. 'Seoras, go back to the safe house with the other car. I'm going to sit with Perry for the rest of the evening and have a few words about what to do and what not to do and how to do it. If you guys are going to act beyond the boundaries that I set, I'm going to need to train you up better.'

'And what? I don't need the training?' said Macleod.

'You're not being put in any of the situations,' she said. 'Trust me, you're the last person I want to see doing the things Perry's doing. Perry's got a fighting chance. You wouldn't have a hope.'

Macleod left and got out of the car. He began to drive off, and Perry turned to Kirsten.

'I think you hurt his feelings with that one.'

'It's important. He needs to know it. He needs to hear it. Seoras wouldn't have a chance. You got up here, and you stayed in the quiet. Until they started sweeping, you were safe. I was watching you,' said Kirsten. 'Your problem is that you got stuck in a situation and didn't know what to do. Well, I'm going to talk to you about that. It's going to be a long rest of the night, so come on, drive, Perry. Let's get going.'

Chapter 13

There had been the tense meeting the night before in the barn, but Hope was up early. In truth, she hadn't slept, only fitfully, and she felt it was just as good an idea to get up and get on the go as it was to go back to bed. The one thing about pregnancy she'd found was she didn't feel overly tired. Maybe she was fortunate in that way.

She felt a lot of other things, but the sickness had been going recently, and in truth, she was doing okay considering she was well along. It wouldn't be that long, another month or two, and she definitely would sit down most of the day, or be waddling her way around the kitchen. She wondered what that was going to be like, with her full-sized bump. She put her hand down, rubbing her belly through her T-shirt.

She hung her coat up inside her own office and then walked to climb the stairs up towards the Chief Constable's office. It was Jim's old office that he had when he was the Assistant Chief Constable, and since the ACC post hadn't been replaced yet, the office was still here. Jim was travelling around a lot more, and whenever he came up to Inverness, he would often use his old office.

Hope walked along past Macleod's office and Tanya's desk

outside it, before arriving at Jim's towards the end of the corridor. She rapped politely on the door, and was told to come in. She entered.

'Sit down,' said Jim quickly, pulling over a chair.

'I'm fine,' said Hope. 'I'm not an invalid. I'm absolutely fine.'

'You shouldn't be in at the moment,' he said. 'If I was your boss—and I know I am your boss, but I'm not your direct boss—if I was Macleod, I would have told you to go. I would have insisted on it. You shouldn't be about here with this going on.'

'Am I safer at home?' asked Hope.

'I kind of hope that they wouldn't harm you because of who you're carrying,' said Jim, 'but who knows with this group.'

'I'm here to update you,' said Hope. 'Seoras can't do it himself, so I'll do it for him.' Hope relayed what had happened over the last few days. She also mentioned that Lady Cockburn seemed to be involved, causing Jim's face to grow serious.

'That's heavy weight, that is,' he said. 'The Cockburns are not just anyone; they're seriously connected. If they're at the heart of this . . .'

'I know,' said Hope. 'But that's who it is.'

'Your team's awfully exposed,' said Jim. 'Very exposed. I'm not happy about it. I'd be happier if Miss Hunt would just come in and take this over. Her people are used to that sort of thing. And they work covertly, harder to spot, harder to . . .'

'She doesn't know that her Service is trustworthy enough for it yet. Anna also didn't have any leads to go on. She knows what Seoras tells her will be true.'

'Is she expecting us to arrest them? I mean, we can do, but you're talking about the Cockburns and trying to make that stick. The legal fight will be immense; there'll be . . . well, after everything, it'll be tough.'

'Trust Macleod and trust Kirsten,' said Hope. 'They need to infiltrate quietly, so let them. Let them do it.'

'I've trusted them this far, haven't I? I'll tell you what worries me, Hope,' said Jim. 'The sympathisers within the force. Somebody passed messages off to someone about Emmett. They passed messages about Clarissa too. There's bad apples in the force. I don't expect that of our people.

'We're all different. You and I are different. I got you wrong once before. You saved a load of people in stopping that bomb from going off. But you know I've always been on the same side. I want to protect the public. That's what I do. It's what you do. This thing of people going behind our back, attacking us in that sense, I don't get it. It worries me. It worries me greatly.'

'I get them,' said Hope, and saw Jim's surprise.

'What do you mean, you get them?'

'Well, I get them,' said Hope, 'because some of these criminals get away with it. Get away with it so much, and then you get somebody who's able to step in and just solve it like that. Brutally. Illegally. Not in the way it should be sorted. But they're taking the bad guys out of the picture. In some ways, the Service is like that.'

'The Service has more controls.'

'You think? But that's what they want. They want somebody to say that we actually got them in the end. We don't always look for the justice side. We just look to say it's sorted. And that's why some of them will co-operate with the Forseti group. However, putting ourselves in danger, putting colleagues in danger, that's a step beyond again.'

'I've got a meeting in about half an hour I've got to prepare for,' said Jim. 'If you hear any more, talk to me. Otherwise, I'll talk with you later this afternoon. And you take care of yourself,' he said to her. 'I mean that. You protect yourself at all costs.'

'I've already had that from Seoras. I wouldn't be here unless I could do my job,' said Hope.

She left his office and walked back down the top corridor. It was quiet at this time of the morning but she saw a constable coming the other way. Hope didn't recognise him, but he was certainly fitted out in a proper police uniform. She saw the numbers on the shoulder, but she stopped anyway.

'Where are you going?' she asked. 'We don't see many constables up on this level. Not at this time of the morning.'

'Just dropping the mail in for the Chief Constable.'

The man held up an envelope to Hope. She looked at it. The man was quite square set, maybe in his late twenties. The envelope had a bulge in it, but it certainly had the name of the Chief Constable on it.

'Very good,' said Hope. She turned and watched the man walk down the corridor. After a bit, Hope turned away. Something, however, was troubling her. As she walked past Macleod's office, she stopped by Tanya's desk and picked up the phone. Hope dialled down to the main desk below, where the post would be sorted and sent out through.

'This is DI Hope McGrath. I've just seen a parcel come up, heading off for the Chief Constable.'

'That's unusual,' said the woman on the phone. 'Because all the Chief Constable's mail is getting routed down to Glasgow. We don't know when he's up here. He never tells us when he comes, so we don't hang on to anything. Here, we send it all away. Hello? Hello?'

Hope had left the phone hanging off the desk, and she was running as hard as she could down the corridor. She wasn't at a stage where she had to waddle, but she was at a stage where running was a lot harder than it used to be. Despite this, she got to the door of the chief constable's office, turned the handle, and threw the door wide open.

In front of her, she saw the constable attacking Jim. Jim had clearly been hurt already, for he was half-doubled over, and blood was coming from his stomach area. The knife went in again, and Hope grabbed the man from behind. He went to spin round, and she twisted as best she could, flinging him away from Jim, who tumbled to the floor.

The man now squared up, knife in hand, towards Hope. He swung at her, and she stepped to one side and he swung again. This time, she stepped inside and caught him with a blow to the chin, knocking him backwards. However, when she went to follow up, she realised he wasn't as stunned as he appeared and he drove the knife straight in towards her gut.

Hope could feel the driving force against her, but she bounced away, much to the man's surprise. He went to drive again, and she reached down, grabbing his hand, and twisted it. She kicked him in the back of the knee, and he went to ground. He came up again, however.

She grabbed his head at this point and drove it hard into the wall three times and the man tumbled down, but he then rolled up again. She punched him twice to the face, but he launched back catching her across the chin. Hope could taste the blood in her mouth and he still had the knife in his other hand as she reeled backwards from the punch.

He dived at her, stabbing her three times in towards her gut each time. His face gave a questioning look as she felt the force and stumbled back before hitting the wall. She regathered herself and, as he came in this time, spun round and, swinging her fist round, caught him across the jaw. This sent him spinning.

Clearly, this one had really hurt him, and she could see he was groggy. As she made to grab him, he instead kicked out at her, catching her in the stomach and sending her backwards. As she hit the wall, she saw him run off as hard as he could.

Hope felt the breath go from her. She reached forward, grabbing her sore belly, but then she looked over and saw the blood on the carpet. There was pooling blood around Jim. She forced herself to stand, get over to the phone, and called downstairs to the desk sergeant.

'Chief Constable's been stabbed. Ambulance, now. Get me first aiders, assistants, now. In his office, now,' she said.

Hope turned back and knelt down beside Jim, pushing him off to one side to see where the bleeding was coming from. She took off her T-shirt, ignoring the fact she was just in her bra now, and placed the T-shirt across his stomach. Pushing down as hard as she could, Hope tried to stop the blood from oozing out. The T-shirt became bloody. Her hands became bloody. And then others arrived.

'Medics are coming,' she heard. Someone took over from her and then there were more people. Someone handed her a coat and wrapped it round her. A hand showed her to a seat. She cradled forward, holding onto her stomach. It was ten minutes later when a paramedic ran in.

They ran over directly to Jim, and soon there were three of them working around him. One other was over with her. The lady knelt before her.

'You're pregnant,' she said.

'Yes,' said Hope. 'I'm pregnant.'

'Have you sustained injury?'

'Hit several times down here,' she said, rolling her hand around her belly. But her mind was on Jim. He was being whipped away now. They were only across from the hospital and he'd be in A&E in five minutes. Had they stabilised him, or did they just need to move him, anyway?

'Is he going to be—?' started Hope.

'Can't say about him. Need to focus on you,' said the woman. 'We need to focus on you.' She could feel the woman's hands now, running across her belly. 'Feels good,' she said from the outside. 'It feels good, but there's no blood on the outside. I'm going to need to have a proper look. Are you able to lie down?'

'Yes,' said Hope. 'They tried to stab me.' She could feel the shock coming on. Hope knew she was speaking quickly, irrationally. 'But it's okay. It's okay. He told me. He told me to take precautions. Seoras said take precautions.'

'Is Seoras your partner?' said the woman.

'No, no. He's my boss. He's my boss.'

Hope could feel herself sweating now. She had sweated during the fight, but this was coming out of nowhere. She should have been easing now, but no. Instead, she could feel it. Her mind was racing. Her body was racing. Everything was on the go.

'Easy,' said the woman. 'Easy.' She lay Hope down, and Hope looked up into faces that she knew from the station looking down.

'Can we get a bit of room here?' said the woman. 'I need to look after my patient. I need people to step back, okay?'

The woman was suddenly talking to another paramedic. Hope could feel her pulse being taken.

'We're going to need to get you checked out,' said the woman. 'I'm going to do an initial one here just to make sure we can move you, that you're okay to go.'

'They didn't get me,' said Hope, laughing suddenly. 'They didn't get me. I'm okay.'

Hope reached down to where her pregnancy jeans came up over her belly. 'Can I have a look?' said the woman.

'Yes,' said Hope. 'Look.' She pulled the pregnancy jeans down and revealed a smile. A small wrap-like contraption.

'What's that?' said the woman.

'It's a stab vest, or at least a stab patch. Knife can't go through it,' said Hope. 'The knife can't go through it.'

The woman looked, then undid it, and took the stab patch away. Her hands ran over Hope's belly. 'Did you get hit here?'

'Yes,' said Hope.

'I can see there's going to be some bruising. There are some marks,' she said, 'but the blade didn't go through. Let's get you to A&E, get you looked after.'

Hope was lifted and taken out, but as she went down the station stairs, she noted Ross appear.

'Hope,' he said, 'Hope, are you all right?'

'Alan,' she said, 'Alan, it worked, it worked.'

The paramedics rushed her out of the building into an ambulance, leaving Ross standing, without a clue as to what was going on, or what Hope meant. And why did she look so incredibly happy?

Chapter 14

Macleod picked up the mobile phone and got a shock when he realised it was Clarissa on the other end. 'I gave these Sim cards to Hope so she could call me, and only to be used in case of emergency, or having to get something to me quickly,' he said.

'Shut up, Seoras,' said Clarissa. 'Listen, Jim's been attacked in his office. He's been knifed. Hope tried to save him. They tried to stab her as well.'

'What?' said Macleod. 'Is she okay? Is she—'

'She's over in the hospital in Raigmore, and she's okay. They're checking the baby.'

'But she got stabbed.'

'No, she had a stab proof patch which protected the baby. But she was damn lucky. Jim wasn't so lucky. He's had several puncture wounds into the stomach. He's in theatre at the moment. Stable, but he's critical.'

Macleod went silent.

'I told you this was coming,' said Clarissa. 'It's open season here. We need action; don't need to be sitting about. We need to actually act on this. Got to close these people down now. We're under threat. I don't care if you get Anna, you get whoever. You have to go after these people. We have to stop them. End them now.'

'Did they say if Jim's going to be okay?' asked Macleod.

'They haven't said. He's critical in hospital. I'm here trying to cover off what Hope would have covered. I've got Susan with me at the moment. Ross too. Emmett and Sabine. We're ready to do whatever you need us to do. But this needs to end fast.'

'I take it John's over with Hope.'

'Yes, we got John there. Ross did it first thing as soon as he knew something was up. Hope's getting the attention she needs. Jim's getting the attention he needs. But we've got a lot more scared team members here. It's like we're just waiting for it. You need to do something, Seoras. You need to move on this now. Because if you don't, I will.'

'And do what?' asked Macleod.

'I don't know. I'll go to Anna Hunt, something, whatever.'

'Stay put,' he said. 'Yes, we need to do something quickly, need to move on this. We need to get this to an end point fast. I agree with you, but I need to know how to do that. So I'm going to talk to Kirsten. I want to see what my options are.'

'Whatever you're going to do, you do it quick, because it's open season here. That's what it feels like. It feels like we're in one of those fairground shooting games. Just moving along to be taken down. I'm not kidding, Seoras. I'm going to do something about this if you don't act soon.'

Macleod signed off in agreement and then broke the Sim card he was using.

'They're getting through an awful lot of the emergency phones,' said Kirsten, suddenly. Macleod looked round to see her there.

'Well, it was important,' he said. 'The Chief Constable's been knifed in his office in Inverness. Hope tried to save him. Hope was attacked too.'

Kirsten stopped for a moment. 'Is she okay?'

'She's okay. They're checking the baby. Jim's in surgery. He's stable, but he's still critical.'

'Okay,' said Kirsten.

'Okay?' said Macleod. 'It's not okay. We're sitting ducks at the moment. They keep coming for us. Somebody's going to end up dead soon.'

'We should wait, get our intelligence so we can go for these people properly. We should be—'

'No,' said Macleod. 'This is not the Service. We don't know how to handle ourselves. We can't stop people from coming in and doing this. Don't you understand? We're not capable of protecting ourselves in the way you would, and Anna can't obviously do it either. Your estimation is not how we see this. We've got people, partners, loved ones, too close to this. No,' said Macleod. 'This ends now. We go on a plan to end this. We go on a plan to accelerate this and get it done.'

'Are you sure that's the right thing to do?' asked Kirsten.

Macleod nodded his head. 'But ask Perry,' he said. 'He'll say the same. He'll say the same as me.'

Kirsten pulled out her phone and contacted Perry, who was sitting watching Lady Cockburn's estate, where she currently was still in residence. Macleod updated him on the current issues.

'They openly attacked the chief constable,' said Perry. 'This has gone beyond. They're coming for us in a big way. It's open season. Absolutely right what they said at the station. It's open season. Now, we need to protect ourselves by getting to the bottom of this now. Otherwise, we won't stop it in time before we lose one of us.'

'Thank you, Perry,' said Macleod.

'Keep him on the line,' said Kirsten, 'because we need to think about what we're going to do.'

'Well, we need to end it quickly. How do we end it quickly?' said Perry.

'Well, we need intelligence about what's going on. There's Lady Cockburn and Malcolm Varney,' said Kirsten. 'We've been planning to watch them, but we could infiltrate. We could find out what they know, but that would involve breaking into both houses.'

'That means Loch Bandaloch then for Lady Cockburn,' said Perry. 'Varney's got a big house on the edge of Inverness. I could take one of them. You could take the boss and go to the other.'

'No, no, no, no,' said Kirsten. 'Nobody is infiltrating on their own. You don't know how to. You don't know how to do it properly and not get caught or leave something behind. I am not letting one of you two head off on your own. It's not happening,' said Kirsten.

'We need to move quickly,' said Macleod. 'You're not going to do two places in one night. That's not going to work, is it?'

'It won't,' agreed Kirsten.

'So, what do I do?' said Macleod.

'Ask Anna for help,' said Kirsten. 'Ask her to send a competent infiltrator to us. Someone that can look after you. You or Perry. Someone like Varney should be fairly easy. I could take the Cockburns. It'll be harder, but I'll take Perry with me for that one.'

'Okay. Talk to Anna then.'

'Can I make another suggestion?' asked Kirsten.

'What?' said Macleod.

'Why don't we bring in Clarissa and Sabine?'

'Clarissa and Sabine? Why? What do we need them for? We're going to bring in one of Anna Hunt's to help us.'

'I want Clarissa with me at Loch Bandaloch,' said Kirsten.

'You were the one who didn't want her in. She's wild, a nutter. She's aggressive, frequently goes off the handle,' said Macleod.

'And she knows her stuff. Inside out. And she understands Forseti Group. She gets all the stuff behind it. If I'm going looking for things, I want to have somebody there who understands what they're looking for. She's from an arts world. She understands the meaning of symbology, the history, all behind it when she was out there in Heligoland with me.

'The likelihood is that Lady Cockburn is the one who's going to have the Forseti background, not Varney, from what we understand. Sabine, we bring in because, one, she's very good at infiltrating,' said Kirsten. 'She has that ability, and she's also got the arts side. She understands the arts side of the Forseti group, and the symbology, and you're going to need that, alongside somebody who knows how to break into a place.'

'And then do what with the rest of them?' said Macleod.

'Hope's down. Patterson's down,' said Perry. 'The obvious thing would be to make Emmett take charge back there. He'll have Ross, Hope, if she comes back out of the hospital. They can work on identifying Varney's interests. See where he's coming from in all of this. Because he's the one we don't understand.

'Cockburn's got a history. The family has history. She's

already involved with the orphanage. She's deep in the Forseti group. Is he? Or is he being used? Or is Varney something outside of the Forseti group? We need to understand that,' said Perry. 'So, let's get Ross on that with Emmett. Hope, when she comes out.'

'Are you sure you want Clarissa? She's a wildfire, could just go off on a tangent. She could blow this completely,' said Macleod.

'I'll take her,' said Kirsten; 'she's needed. You forget I've handled her before. She scared the living daylights out of herself last time. And besides, she's much more likely to do something wild away from us than she is with us. If she sees things happening, if she sees action on the go, then maybe, just maybe, she'll work with us and stay within the rules.'

'You don't know her that well, do you?' said Macleod. But he gave his agreement anyway. 'Thanks, Perry. We'll be in touch,' he said. And then he told Kirsten he'd have to phone Anna Hunt.

Anna Hunt had a few special lines she could be contacted on and Macleod dialled one of these. It rang for all of two minutes before he heard a familiar voice on the end of the line.

'Hello, there, Detective Chief Inspector,' said Anna. 'You've called on the private line.'

'I need your assistance. You said you'd be willing to help with this one.'

'I heard Jim was rushed to the hospital. I'm sorry,' she said. 'You need to get a move on.'

'I know I need to get a move on,' said Macleod. 'Hope's gone in as well.'

'Is she okay?'

'She was knifed, but she had a stab vest. A stab protector

that was across her belly. Saved the wee one.'

'Well, that is good news,' said Anna. 'What do you need from me?'

'I can't hang about and I need to get inside two houses. There's only one Kirsten here. I need someone from your people to come and help me. Somebody good at breaking in. It's an edge of the city, large house. Malcolm Varney.'

'Just a moment,' said Anna.

Macleod waited on the end of the phone, wondering what on earth the woman could be doing but she came back three minutes later.

'Sending them up on the train. You'll meet them off this evening's train and you'll take them to the house. Is it just yourself going in with them?'

'I'm going to bring Sabine as well.'

'Good,' said Anna. 'She's Service material; do you know that?'

'You're not taking her to be like you and Kirsten.'

'That sounds like a slur. Not wise to give that to somebody who's trying to help you.'

'You forget,' said Macleod, 'you're the one being helped. You're the one whose Service can't deal with this. And you have put all of my team in jeopardy because you won't take over and sort it. So, this is not you doing a favour to me; this is you helping to sort out your own mess.'

'Easy,' said Anna suddenly. 'You need to calm down. You need to get yourself thinking straight.'

'Well, which bit of it isn't true?' said Macleod.

'What is true or not about the situation isn't important. What is important is you are calm and thinking through the situation. I am not sending one of my people up tonight to have you go off half-cocked.'

'You just send your person up here. Make sure they're good.'

'They'll be adequate for the job. I'll tell them to keep an eye on you as well. You can't lose it in the middle of this, Seoras. Just because things have got rough, you can't lose it. Think straight. Look at Kirsten. She doesn't flinch; she thinks straight.'

'Tonight,' said Macleod, 'make sure they're there. What time's the train?'

'Eight o'clock,' said Anna. 'And you'll have calmed down by then.'

Macleod came off the phone and turned to face Kirsten. 'She's sending somebody up on the eight o'clock train. I'll pick them up with Sabine,' said Macleod. 'You do yours with Perry and Clarissa. I'll phone her and tell her the good news.'

'I'll do that. I've got a lot to talk to her about. Set her up. Make sure she doesn't go off half-cocked.'

'Ask about Hope when you do it.'

Kirsten nodded and then stopped. 'There's nobody else here,' she said. 'What was it with you and Hope? You always . . . you had something beyond being partners. You weren't just a team.'

'You were always like the daughter I never had,' Macleod said to Kirsten. 'You had it tough, your brother to look after. But you think like me. In some ways, apart from the fact you're stronger, fitter, and possibly a lot more cunning, you are like me. I understood you.

'Hope's never been like me. Hope has intrigued me since the start.' Macleod stood up. 'What else Hope and me are to each other, and what we share, that's between Hope and me. You hear anything, any news, tell me straight away.'

He could feel Kirsten watching him as he left the room, but he was going to go now and lie down for an hour. Everything was happening so fast. The pressure was ramping up, and he needed, above all, to chill out. What he needed was Jane. Jane could always break through. But Jane wasn't here. And neither would she be until this was all over.

Chapter 15

Clarissa stood at the end of the street, dressed in unfamiliar black. She had a shawl on, but it was reversed inside out, for the other side was garish and bright. On her head, she wore a beanie black hat, and when Perry almost drove past her, she thought she'd got it right. Realising his error, he picked her up and took her to Kirsten's safe house. On arrival, Clarissa stepped inside to a modest lounge, and saw Kirsten, deep in her notebooks.

'Kirstie,' she said. Kirsten looked up and glared at her.

'You wanted to work? It's time to work,' said Kirsten.

'What are we doing?' asked Clarissa.

'We go to infiltrate Cockburn's tonight, the estate, and into his main house.'

'Okay, and you want me to give you a rundown on what you can expect?'

'No,' said Kirsten. 'You're coming with me.'

'What? Why do you want me with you?'

'Because, for all that you're not, you understand this Forseti group, or at least a lot around them. You'll be able to identify things of substance, of note. And that's why you're with me. Perry will watch the house from the outside.'

Clarissa gulped. 'We're going in on reconnaissance.'

'Yes,' said Kirsten. 'But this time we go in silent, and we come out silent. We don't disturb anything.'

'Okay,' said Clarissa. Perry made a cup of coffee for everyone before they sat down and discussed details about how the plan would work. Kirsten advised Macleod she wasn't happy that she was going in without having watched the place for a couple of nights, but she was confident she could handle it.

There's no choice, Kirstie, we need to be on this,' said Clarissa. 'We need to get going. We can't wait for the intel. A couple of days, who knows who they'll come for. We haven't all got fists and wits like you,' said Clarissa.

'Just keep your wits about you when you're in there,' said Kirsten. She'd pulled out some maps of the estate, and together they planned how they would enter. They were coming in from quite a distance out, but Clarissa said she was up to it. She wasn't quick, but she could go the distance.

'You'll watch from here, Perry. Binoculars, make sure we get in. Any trouble, I want you to come over here in the car. That's where we'll get to, and where you'll extract us from.'

Clarissa watched as Kirsten checked the equipment she had with her, her flashlight, various little gizmos that she attached into a belt around her waist. Then she checked her gun.

'That's coming with us, is it?' asked Clarissa.

'Yes, it is. Just for me, since you don't know how to use one. I'm not planning on using it, but if push comes to shove . . .'

Macleod's team departed to pick up their infiltrator leaving Kirsten's team to rest before their op. Once midnight had come, they left the house, Perry driving them to the drop-off point. The estate wasn't overly well-protected, and Kirsten had chosen a broken-down piece of wall to get through. While it was a distance from the main house, it at least provided easy access. She didn't fancy scaling walls with Clarissa. Clarissa was glad that she merely had to swing her leg up and over a small, broken piece of wall.

'Stay close,' said Kirsten, 'and no noise!'

Together, they crept across the grass and approached the side of the main house. Kirsten had decided to go in via a servant's entrance, or at least that's what it must have been intended for in the original building. Getting to the door, she found it locked, picked it, and stepped inside quickly.

The interior was dark, and Kirsten held her hand out behind her, allowing Clarissa to take hold of it and follow her along a passageway. As they got to the end of it, Kirsten stopped.

'Quiet,' she whispered.

Clarissa could hear someone on the other side of the door at the end of the passageway, walking along what must have been a hall or a corridor with a wooden floor. Kirsten braced herself at the door in case it opened, but the footsteps disappeared off again.

Quietly, Kirsten opened the door, and they stepped out into a lighted hallway. From the plans, they knew they had to circle round, going through a corridor and a hallway that was rarely used, or at least that's what they surmised. There was little noise in the house, for most people in the house would be sleeping.

They were just about to move upstairs to where Lord Cockburn and his wife would sleep when Perry announced to their earpieces that Lady Cockburn had left. Kirsten tapped her ear twice to show to Perry that she'd understood the message. She snuck up the stairs, a marble staircase that went to the upper floor. Here there was little sound. Kirsten stole along before opening one door into an extensive office.

Kirsten pointed around, and Clarissa hastened through everything that was there, gently putting it back afterwards.

'Are we seeing anything?' whispered Kirsten.

'Don't believe so. Nothing at all.'

'Blast it,' said Kirsten.

She went to go through another door, but bent down and looked through the keyhole. There was a light on in the room next door. Carefully, Kirsten put a tiny wire with a camera on the end through the hole. She held in her hand a tiny screen, and it showed that someone was sitting in a study.

Slowly, Kirsten drew the device back out, indicating to Clarissa they couldn't go that way. Instead, they went back out of the door they had entered through, moved down the corridor past that room, and into what was a bedroom. Again, they searched up and down and round it, but there was nothing. Kirsten pulled Clarissa further along and into a blacked-out bedroom with no one in it.

Here she asked her, 'Are you seeing anything? Any indication of Forseti? Anything untoward?'

'Nothing,' said Clarissa. 'Nothing. I'm recognising some portraits and that, but they're nothing to do with Forseti Group. Maybe we're in the wrong place,' said Clarissa. 'Maybe they stored it all somewhere else.'

'Then we'll have to search further.'

They continued through the rest of the upper floor of the house, moving through bedrooms and rooms that were unoccupied, but nowhere was there anything. Kirsten then led their way back round to find Lord Cockburn had left his room and was now in his main bedroom. Taking Clarissa inside the room he'd been sitting in, they once again pored over items until Clarissa stopped.

'What?' mouthed Kirsten. Clarissa pointed. In one drawer, there was a piece of paper. It had a symbol on it. Wavy lines and squiggles, but it meant nothing to Kirsten.

'Nordic. That's a Forseti symbol,' said Clarissa. 'Can't see anything else in here.'

Quickly, the pair made their way downstairs, searching the rest of the quarters. There were several rooms they couldn't go into because servants were asleep in them. Others were just dining rooms, with nothing of particular note. The library was a fascinating collection of books, except none of them had anything to do with Forseti. *Were they just clever enough not to keep anything here?*

There was a sudden movement on the lower floor, and a couple of servants came along. Kirsten grabbed Clarissa, opened a door and backed into it. When she shut it behind her, she realised there were stacks of shelves all around. They moved quietly to the rear of it.

It was a pantry. Jars of flour, eggs, and all sorts of foodstuffs were there. Kirsten told Clarissa to get down, and she listened to hear if anyone would pass by. Someone was outside, probably whoever had come along and disturbed them initially. So, Kirsten showed they should wait. The light then came on in the pantry as the door opened.

There was a man in a chef's outfit, and he looked along the rows. He was getting closer and closer towards Clarissa. Then he turned to go down one set of shelves in the pantry. Kirsten was at the far end of them. Clarissa, seeing where he was going, stood up and ran up behind him, grabbing a rolling pin off a shelf and battered him in the back of the head. The man dropped to the ground.

'What the hell are you doing?' hissed Kirsten.

'He was going to see you,' said Clarissa, 'was heading down your alley here. He would have seen you!'

'No, he would not have seen me. I can move quicker than that. You've just given the game away.' Kirsten was looking all round her now, wondering what she could do.

'I was saving your neck, Kirstie. Don't forget it.'

'He's a baker. He's in looking for ingredients. I can handle the kitchen staff,' said Kirsten.

She looked around, and then saw at the top of one set of shelves some scales. She took them and dropped them with some weights around the man. Grabbing the rolling pin, Kirsten placed it back where it had come from, wiping it clean. The chef was out cold and Kirsten moved some shelves so they'd lie against each other as if something had toppled over.

'We're just going to have to hope that it holds for us. You are an idiot,' said Kirsten. 'You could have got us both killed. Come on.'

As they went to leave, Clarissa suddenly stopped. 'These cookie cutters, they're custom,' said Clarissa.

'We don't need to admire the kitchenware.'

'We do. Those are symbols. They're all for Forseti. They're all to do with the group.'

'Cookie cutters,' said Kirsten. 'They must be at the centre of it. You wouldn't have cookie cutters for the symbols.'

'Don't ask me,' said Clarissa. 'I'm just telling you what's there.'

Carefully, they backtracked out of the pantry, and made their way round to the front of the house. Kirsten decided she needed to scan the estate more and headed out to some of the surrounding buildings. Most were locked, but it wasn't a problem for Kirsten to open them and have a look.

It took them most of the night, but Kirsten went through every building within half a mile of the main house. As they came back over the wall, out to where Perry was waiting, she said to him,

'Nothing. Nothing. A couple of indications that it's the Forseti group. Things like cookie cutters and small drawings. Nothing else. Nothing to say that their base is here. Nothing to give any indication what's going on.'

'Were you expecting them to?' said Perry. 'The last thing I would do is fill my house if I was running a secret organisation.'

'Usually, they have it somewhere within the house. Store it there. It's easier to have it close than try to maintain locations away. They know who's coming on to the estate, and are able to watch. Genuine reasons.'

'A fair point,' said Perry, 'but no luck.'

'They must have something somewhere close though,' said Clarissa. 'These people worship their stone circles. You will not travel to Heligoland every time you wanted to do a ceremony or kill someone.'

'But they killed out in the open before.'

'That was for us, Perry,' said Clarissa, 'this is for them, so I don't understand why there isn't somewhere, somewhere close.'

'Well, there might be,' said Kirsten. 'We don't know the buildings around the main estate. There may be other places close at hand. Did Lady Cockburn come back?' she asked Perry.

'No, I'm not sure where she's gone.'

'Dirty stop out,' said Clarissa. 'Strange though if the Cock-burns are in cahoots for Forseti together, if that's what they're at, that he would let her disappear off like that.'

'Who knows?' said Perry. 'Who knows?'

As they got into the back of the car, letting Perry drive them back, Kirsten felt Clarissa tap her on the shoulder.

'Sorry,' said Clarissa. 'I overreacted. With everything that's gone on lately, I thought he was going for you. I wasn't going to let him take you out.'

'It's why I said you shouldn't be here,' said Kirsten. 'I said I needed you. And now that we've upped the speed of the investigation, I need you more to spot things when we're inside. But you need to relax.'

'How do you relax when people are trying to kill you?'

'Trust me,' said Kirsten. 'It makes you think a lot better. It makes you think a whole lot smoother.'

'Well, the red mist has got me out of plenty of occasions,' said Clarissa. 'I always have to remember that. Sometimes you have to be what you are.'

Kirsten shook her head. 'You need to be what you need to be in whatever situation you're in. That's the important bit,' said Kirsten.

'I'm here without a shawl or tartan trews. I've taken away my identity to do this. Just be thankful for that,' said Clarissa.

Kirsten shook her head in the back seat. It had been a long night. She was ready for bed.

Chapter 16

Macleod stood on the platform at Inverness Station, awaiting Anna's contact. He was in an unusual raincoat and jeans, which, for him, was something that just didn't happen, and a beanie hat. His false beard was agitating him, too. He watched as the train rolled in, came to a stop, and he made sure he was standing at the third carriage along. The doors opened and people flooded out, but no one came towards him. The travellers passed along the platform down to the exit barriers and Macleod thought he was on his own. He went to turn away when he heard a voice.

'You looking for company, all on your own?'

Macleod turned around and saw a dark-haired woman underneath a broad hat. He couldn't see the eyes, but the shape was right. The head tilted up and then Anna Hunt looked back at him.

'I said I wanted assistance. You didn't have to come yourself.'

'I did,' she said. 'You're going in inside somebody else's house. I can't have that going wrong. Not you. Kirsten will look after the others. But somebody needs to look after you, Seoras.'

She strode forward and put her arm through Macleod's. 'Walk like we know each other.'

'We do know each other,' said Macleod.

'Yes, but not in a professional context. Make it out like you're glad to see me.'

He felt her pull at his arm and drag him down the platform. Over her other shoulder was a large bag and Macleod didn't want to ask what she had inside of it. Instead, he walked with her and then led her out to where the car was parked before driving her to the safe house.

'We don't have a lot of time. The other team's already prepped to go out,' said Macleod. 'Varney's house is on the edge here of Inverness.'

Sabine placed some photographs down on the table, preparations for the entry that she'd been doing while Macleod picked up Anna.

'This should be easy enough,' said Anna. 'I'm doing most of it on the hoof. One thing I have to say, though, is I dictate what happens here.' Anna was staring at Macleod now.

'You got that, Sabine?' Macleod said.

'I have no worries about her,' said Anna. 'Sabine will be outside watching us. You, however, I need inside.'

'Why?' asked Macleod. 'Sabine knows more about the symbology of the Forseti group.'

'I don't want you on the outside as my escape route,' said Anna. 'Kirsten tells me Sabine can think on her feet. Kirsten tells me she's athletic, can handle herself. Last thing we need is you standing out there in a car and getting lifted by just anybody.'

'You talk like I'm the old man of this operation,' said Macleod.

'Well, frankly, you are,' said Anna. 'You've got the brains, Seoras. But when it comes to being dynamic, being someone to put your trust in to get you out of a situation, I'm taking my bets on Sabine.'

Macleod looked over and thought that Sabine was suppressing a smile. Anna disappeared into another room and came back dressed in black. She took out a gun, checked it, put it away, then checked the several knives she wore as well. She looked up to see the alarm on Macleod's face.

'We could be going into the lion's den here,' said Anna. 'I'm coming out. Whatever happens, I'm coming out.'

'You think I should be armed as well,' said Macleod. 'I'm not doing that. I'm a police officer, I'm not—'

'You're not going to be armed,' said Anna Hunt. 'The last thing I'm going to do is give a gun to somebody that doesn't know what to do with it.'

'Come on,' said Sabine, 'we should really get going. It's after midnight.'

Anna nodded, and the team quickly made their way out, driving to just beyond Varney's house. It was a large building, but not the grand house of an estate, such as Lady Cockburn had. This was more modern. It had glass windows down one side. Anna decided they would pop over from the rear of the house and approach it that way. Most of the house was in darkness, but she spotted that there were lights on the outside.

'We go through there,' she said, pointing. 'Along this path here. We won't get surveillance lights coming on walking that route. I'll see what I can do about switching them off.'

Anna was away without a word. Macleod worked hard to keep up with Anna Hunt, marvelling at how, for her age, she was still so athletic. He wondered if she could keep up with Kirsten. After all, there were several years between them. But he didn't have time to think about that, as he worked hard just to keep within her wake.

She approached the house, and then disappeared round the side, before coming back to advise Macleod the lights would no longer be working outside. Anna stepped up to the rear door, saw it was alarmed, and attached a small device to the side of it. She opened the door, and then at a pace, made for a main panel of the alarm in the hall. Macleod saw her tamper with the device. Anna then waved Macleod to be with her, and they stopped, holding their breath, in the main hallway.

Anna pointed up with her finger, showing somebody was still awake. Quickly, they stole upstairs and identified the door from which the voice coming from. They could hear someone standing up from a chair, and Anna looked around her quickly. She grabbed the door of another bedroom, opened it, and took Macleod inside. The room was dark, and Macleod could see a teenage girl asleep on her bed. Anna closed the door quickly behind her and then listened.

After a time, Anna opened the door of the young girl's bedroom, bolted across the hall and into the room that the sounds had emanated from. She'd clearly decided whoever was in there had left. When Macleod went to follow her, she turned and waved him back.

He closed the door almost completely, leaving himself just enough of a gap to see out. The door to the other room was wide open, and he could see Anna. She was racing around the room, looking at different things. And then there was a sound of someone coming back.

Macleod watched as he went back into the room where Anna Hunt was. Macleod was ready for a shouting match, for Anna to take him out, to do something. But he saw the man sit down as he failed to close the door behind him. The man had a headset on and began talking to someone.

'Get the bitch. Do it. Need to get the bitch.'

Macleod wondered who he was talking about. Varney continued to talk for another ten minutes. Then he got up and left the room again. Macleod saw Anna Hunt then get out from her hiding place, wherever it was, and start waving him through.

He gingerly opened the door of the bedroom and looked down the corridor. Macleod couldn't see Varney, so he closed the door gently behind him and ran through to the other room. He went to close the door of that room, but Anna stopped him. In the quietest voice he'd ever heard her use, she said,

'He didn't close it. You don't close it. You don't do what they don't do.'

He watched as she turned, and then approaching a bookcase, she pulled down one of the books, and the bookcase slid back. There was a narrow corridor. Anna waved Macleod through. On entering, the bookcase slid back behind them, and together the pair raced into a small office. As Macleod looked around it, he could see a desk with paper scattered on it, a computer on one side, but in the middle, there was a mock-up of what looked like a Forseti stone circle. Anna was knelt down beside it.

'Now that's interesting,' she said. 'Don't you think?'

'Why has he got a model of it? What's he going to do with a model?'

'You tell me. You're here for the brains, not the brawn, remember?' said Anna.

Macleod studied the model and saw there were two names attached to it. Loch Lee, and also Loch Badanloch.

'Badanloch. Loch Badanloch's up by Cockburn's estate. That's where Cockburn is. The house is close to Badanloch.'

'Well, they built one of these at Loch Lee,' said Anna.

'You don't think they're building another one?'

'Well, it is a stone circle. It is for Forseti, isn't it?'

'No doubt,' said Macleod. He took out his mobile phone and began taking photographs of the interior of the room. Anna went straight over to the desk and began photographing all the papers that were on it. And then she held up her hand suddenly.

'What?' whispered Macleod.

She pointed back down the corridor that they'd come through from the bookcase. Slowly, and with her gun drawn, she walked up to the bookcase. But she didn't operate the mechanism. Instead, she stood there, listening. After a minute, she came back and crouched beside Macleod in the office.

'He's back in,' she said. 'We're not going anywhere for a while, so make yourself comfortable. If he comes through, what do you want me to do?'

'What do you mean?' asked Macleod.

'What do you want me to do? Do you want me to take him out so we get out? Are you going to arrest him?'

'You know fine well, I can't arrest him. We've just broken into his house.'

'So, what do we do?' asked Anna. 'Do you want to be dead or alive? Do I take him somewhere?'

'What do you mean, take him somewhere?'

'We can take him back to the safe house, work out what to do with him. See if he'll confess to any names.'

'I don't think he will,' said Macleod. 'Besides, we hold him and they'll cut the ties. They might even cut Lady Cockburn out of the picture. We end up with nothing. We need to come out of here without him knowing.'

'Well, that's down to him,' said Anna. 'Because he's in there. If he walks in here, I'm not sure even I could hide in this place for a minute.'

'But you hid in the other one.'

'I did, but there was a lot more to hide behind in there. And besides, I didn't have you.'

'Well, you're the one who wanted me here.'

'Be useful. I'm going to have to watch the door. You find out what all this stuff is.'

Macleod nodded, but his heart was thumping at the thought of being trapped in here and someone being on the outside. He tried to focus on the paperwork that was on the desk in front of him. There were orders for shipments. It seemed that the stone circles had been moved. There was paperwork that didn't say where it was going, but there was money paid over. Names of people who shipped the stone circles, all neatly presented, ready to be handed over by the look of it.

This was the Forseti group tracking who they were dealing with. This was a way to understand how to cut off the arm if it became compromised. Macleod wondered, had they built another one then? The one in Loch Lee had been made with plastic stones, but would they do another one in such a fashion? Heligoland had been compromised, and they seemed to like their circle.

Macleod wondered if they used it a lot. Was it how they met at the top? After all, they were getting to the top now. And Forseti, the Norse god, was central to their beliefs. It was madness, though, wasn't it? Utter madness. How could you follow something like this? How could you be so brutal with people?

He thought back to his former partner, and how this had all

started with Isbister's death. His innocent death was what had brought Macleod into it all. Initially, back then, and then later, when Emmett had dug up what had happened at Macleod's request.

Macleod suddenly felt a tap on his shoulder, and Anna Hunt put a finger up to her mouth, showing Macleod should be quiet. She then indicated he should follow her up the corridor and stand at the bookcase door. When he got there, he could hear Varney talking to someone again.

'If you have had the opportunity. Take it,' he said.

Macleod wondered what he was talking about. Anna gave a questioning look, but Macleod shook his shoulders. He didn't know what was happening, and Varney had gone quiet. He stayed quiet for the next couple of minutes, and then he suddenly said,

'Good, good! Get out of there, good work.'

Macleod looked across at Anna, who once again shook her shoulders, having no idea what was happening. Then they heard Varney laugh. He was laughing hard, and then he said to the air, 'Take that, you red-headed bitch.'

Macleod's heart sank. Redhead? Something had happened to the redhead. Hope? He thought it could be Hope. He reached for his phone and messaged as quickly as he could.

Chapter 17

Hope McGrath stood at the end of the hospital bed and brushed her hair. She was feeling very lucky after the knife attack and, although she had some minor bruising across her belly, the young one inside her was perfectly fine. That couldn't be said for Jim. He had suffered badly and although he was stable, they still felt he was critical.

Hope had popped up to visit him that day, but now she was about to go home. They said they could keep her in another night but despite the hour, Hope told John she wanted to go home. Everything was so rough at the moment. Everything was full on. She needed a night with her man. She wanted her own bed and to cuddle up.

Hope pulled on her pregnancy jeans, hauled her t-shirt over her head and then dressed in the long coat that was able to wrap around her bump. She smiled to the mirror.

She hadn't heard from the teams. They wouldn't say. She was out of action, hadn't come out of the hospital, but she knew somebody would be there. Emmett, Clarissa, Ross? Somebody would take the lead and keep the contact with Seoras. But for tonight, she would forget about them. For tonight, she would spend a little time with John, and she would sleep.

She heard the door of the room open and recognised the footsteps that sprinted across to her. She felt his arms wrap around her. Then a voice said in her ear, 'How's the sexiest mum to be?' She leaned back and kissed him on the lips. They stayed like that for a moment, enjoying each other, before he asked her was she ready to go.

'We are,' she said. 'We are ready.' John was almost giddy with excitement. He'd had such a shock and Hope could understand it. She always wondered how it felt to him, being on the sidelines when she charged in. It was quite the reversal for a man, she thought. If ever they were attacked, she would be better at defending them than he would.

He picked up her stuff, and she followed him out of the room down to the nurse's station where she said farewell, having been given the all-clear by the doctor to leave a few hours earlier. She had taken her time, and now it was late.

'Shall we go home?' John asked.

'No,' said Hope. 'I don't know what chance we'll get together in the next couple of days. I'll go back in tomorrow. There's bound to be somewhere still open, a curry house or somewhere.'

John smiled. 'I think we can find somewhere.'

They drove into the middle of Inverness and found one of their favourite curry houses. At half past ten, they were given a table. It would remain open, possibly to midnight or just after, but Hope wasn't worried about that. She just wanted something to eat in the company of John. They spent the next hour and a half there. Hope, taking in the wonderful smells, tried not to feel self-conscious as John watched her the whole time. He must be worried, she thought, about the both of us. It can't be easy for him.

She felt at times like she should pick up her phone and find out what was going on, but she was determined to give these couple of hours to John, not to let the job take it away. The job was always taking her away. She wondered how this was going to work when she was a mum.

'Hope,' said John. 'I've been thinking.'

'Well, don't do that too often. Gets you into trouble, that does.'

He gave a half grin, but she knew something serious was coming.

'Look, when the little one gets here, and after you've had your maternity, we need to work out how this is going to work. Somebody's got to look after them. Or they've got to go into nursery or that.'

'I could take up to a year,' said Hope.

'That's what I want to talk about,' said John. 'As a mum, you're going to want to do certain things. You need to decide and tell me if you're going to feed the baby, if they're going to be bottle fed, how long you want to be around our little one.'

'Why?' asked Hope. 'What's bringing this on all of a sudden?'

'Well, we need to make plans. We haven't really made plans, have we? Not good plans. We haven't even got a cot up in the house yet.'

'No, we haven't,' said Hope. I just keep getting caught up in case after case. I keep—'

'That's what I'm talking about.'

Hope stopped for a moment. 'Are you leading on to asking me to give it up? The work?'

John leaned forward and took Hope's hands in his. 'No,' he said. 'You couldn't. I'm amazed we got this kid coming. I'm amazed you want this kid. You are a detective, through and through. You are the female Seoras. Always there for the job. Always there to find the next bad person.'

'I'm sorry,' she said.

'No,' said John. 'It's a good thing. It's who you are. And I know you're going to be a great mum and you're going to try to give the time, but you will be pushed and pulled here and there.'

'So, what are you saying?' asked Hope. 'That I should make some sort of decision? That I should step back or I should—'

'No,' said John. 'I'm thinking, now you're a DI, in terms of money, it's not a problem. We can live on your income.'

'Why? Something wrong with the car place? Is it taking over? Is it in trouble?'

'It's absolutely fine,' said John. 'But I was thinking maybe I could quit it. I would give you the stability in the house. You wouldn't be desperately thinking I have to get back all the time. I was thinking, once you're through your maternity, and we get the baby through those early months, first year, whatever it is, that I step down, and I look after the house.'

Hope looked across at him. 'But that would be you just giving up your career. I mean, you've done well. You're managing the place. You're—'

'Let's be truthful,' said John. 'How many more kids are we going to have? How are we going to make it fit in? Do we really want to have a family where they go off into care all the time? I don't. I don't want a child sitting there thinking that mum and dad are not here. Somebody's got to be there with them and somebody's got to be able to take care of the other stuff. So the one who's working can get to spend time with them as well.'

'But that's your work. That's who you are.'

'No, it's not who I am,' said John. 'I work in the car-hire company, I manage it. Yes, it's great. I get on well with the people. But it's not who I am. You, however, tell me you'd walk away from the job.'

Hope nodded. 'You're right, I couldn't. I wouldn't. I can't.'

'We didn't really think about this,' said John. 'It's crazy. We're having a kid and we didn't think about it. But I have thought about it. You need that stability to come back to. So I'm going to give you it.'

She reached forward with both hands, took his cheeks in them, pulled them close, and kissed him deeply. When they parted, she continued to hold his face.

'That's why I love you,' she said. 'You can do things I can't. You're more than me.'

'You're going to get soppy on me now,' he said. 'Are we agreed then? This is what we do. You tell me how long you want to stay. One year before you go back to work? That's your call. I know it depends on lots of different things, but you tell me, okay?'

Hope now stared at John for the rest of the meal, and when they left, she was buoyed, despite the situation they were in, and the way the Forseti group had come after the team.

They left the curry house late at night, and Hope suggested they go for a short walk. She took John's arm and felt like she could walk a hundred miles with him that night, she was so happy. Taking his arm, they strolled down by the river.

Although it was late at night and past midnight, there were still people on the go. Inverness wasn't like London or one of the larger cities where there was a constant group of people through the night. But it didn't go that quiet. There were still people leaving clubs, bars, night crews on the job. And

Hope enjoyed walking by the river, hearing the rush of water in the dark. They walked down towards Eden Park, routed round the river down there, and then made their way back up towards the city centre.

As they were doing so, Hope noticed somebody. Just at the edge of her view, she spotted someone else on the other side of them. Then she looked up ahead. There was a group of four men there.

'John,' she said suddenly. 'I don't want to alarm you, but we're being followed. Worse than that, we're being surrounded.'

'What do you want to do?' he said under his breath. 'Do we run? Where can we run to?'

They were down by the river, far out of sight of most of the roads.

'We need to get to somewhere where there's people,' said Hope. 'I'll take the first one that comes near us, but I think we should run before that.'

Hope took another couple of steps, then grabbed John's hand and said, 'Run.' She tore off back towards where the busier streets would be, but two men stepped out in front of her. Hope ran into them, driving her shoulder in towards one. She hit him, but he got tangled up with her, and her legs caught in his.

Hope fell hard to the ground, and John toppled over the top of her. She watched John get up, but a man smacked him across the face hard. He fell backwards. Hope drove a fist into the stomach of the man she was with. Four other men now arrived.

She felt a kick in the back. Then another one. Hope bit the leg in front of her, hard. Then she was kicked again. Her hands flew down to cover her belly.

Hope was battered, repeatedly. She wanted to defend John, wanted to scream out. But all she could do was grunt as they hit her. There must have been at least six of them, if not more.

She heard John cry out. One man held John's bloodied head up so Hope could see it and then bounced it back down on the ground. For the next couple of minutes, they kicked her. Harder and harder, until she could barely keep her arms in front of her at all. She took a couple of piercing blows into the stomach. Eventually, it was like everything went dark.

The path away from the river became quiet. In the minutes that followed, the men disappeared.

* * *

James had just been out with friends, and was walking back by the river path, focusing carefully on the ground in front of him. He was swaying from side to side and that was why he didn't react quickly when he saw two figures lying prone on the floor.

One had long red hair, the other was a man who looked slightly shorter than her, but neither of them were moving. As James half staggered over, he saw that the phone of one of them was lying out on the ground. It was illuminating now, and he knelt down beside it. It was a text message of some sort, from someone called Macleod.

James looked at the woman. She had a stomach, quite large, and then he realised she was pregnant. She also was bleeding from the mouth. The man was bleeding too. James reached down for his own phone. It took him two goes to try to unlock it. But then he dialled 999.

'Which Service do you require?'

'There's someone here. They've been beaten up.'

'Where are you? Do you need the ambulance? Is it an ambulance or police?'

'Both!' said the man. He hiccupped, almost in a surreal state.

'Ambulance Service.'

'Hi, um, two people beaten up. Need help. She's pregnant.'

'Is she breathing?'

'I think so. She's not conscious. Neither of them are conscious. Hang on.' James reached down and put his hand in front of her face.

'She's breathing a bit, I think.'

'Where are you?' the woman asked.

'Oh, hell,' said the man. 'I don't know. Eh.'

'Will your phone tell you?'

The man said, 'Yes. I know.' He looked at the phone and pressed the button for the compass. 'It's got numbers here.'

'Read them out to me,' said the woman.

About two minutes later, the man sat down on the ground. They had told him to wait, the ambulance was on its way. He looked over at the woman and the man. Should he be doing something? Well, he didn't know. He hiccupped again. What were they doing out here? *Crazy*, he thought. *Just crazy.*

Chapter 18

Clarissa and Kirsten had made their way back to the safe house and were awaiting Macleod and Anna, who had been delayed. According to a message from Anna, they were stuck in the house waiting for Varney to exit a room so they could get out. However, they'd also sent a disturbing message through that they thought someone had been attacked by Varney, possibly Hope.

Having got back to the house, Clarissa thought she should check. She tried to call Hope but got no answer. Next, she contacted Emmett to see if he knew, and it had taken him a few hours to track down that Hope was in the hospital with John. She'd been rushed into Accident and Emergency. They were both a mess, and although John was seriously battered, they felt he would survive okay. But they were more worried about Hope. She'd taken the brunt of the blows, and they'd also battered her around her midriff. Hope was giving the doctors grave concern.

Emmett had dispatched Susan to stay down at the hospital and not only co-ordinate protection for Hope, but also to monitor how she was. Kirsten had decided not to inform Macleod yet, not until Anna and he could get out on their own.

She didn't want them compromised. If Macleod thought Hope was in hospital, he might push Anna into trying to leave early, instead of waiting it out until Varney disappeared.

It was still quite early in the morning when Perry called up Kirsten, advising that Cockburn had come home. As far as Perry could tell, she hadn't gone to bed yet, but was waiting up. Kirsten grabbed Clarissa and headed back out to meet up with Perry. When they parked up beside him, he got out of his car, and came over with a pair of binoculars.

'I think something interesting's happening,' he said.

'How do you mean?' asked Kirsten.

'She's come back from her night out, but she's stayed up. From what I can see, she's gone from room to room. She's come downstairs, she's gone upstairs. He's up, Lord Cockburn. He's moving about as well, and she seems to avoid all the rooms he's in. Now, this is a premise, but I think she's waiting for him to get out of the way.'

'You deduced all that just from standing out here with a pair of binoculars,' said Clarissa.

'Well, think about it,' said Kirsten. 'He's right. Been out all night. Even if you've been out all night with someone, you're going to want to come back and go to bed. You will not keep out of the way. She might be waiting to do something.'

'So, what does that mean?' said Clarissa. 'We went in. We found nothing of great use, did we?'

'No, we didn't,' said Kirsten. 'But hold your horses. Think about what Seoras and Anna have just done. They found Varney's secret place. We found no one's secret place in there.'

'And?' said Clarissa.

'Well, if she's dancing about during the day, if she's avoiding her husband, maybe that's because she's wanting to go to her secret place.'

'You think she's not involved in it with him? He's not part of it?' asked Clarissa.

'Not necessarily,' said Perry, interjecting. 'Think about how the Forseti group works, the way they cut off the arms, how they make sure that the central person is protected. Maybe he's the central person. It would be strange that she would be aligned with the orphanage if she was the central person. You wouldn't make that connection. You wouldn't compromise yourself like that. So maybe what is secret for her doesn't go to him. Maybe lots of her contacts are not known to him. Is the orphanage known to him? Maybe how she sets things up is to keep separate from him.'

'Seriously,' said Clarissa. 'Sounds like a lot of work to me.'

'This could be an opportunity.'

'How, Kirstie?' asked Clarissa.

'If she's waiting for him to be out of the way, she'll make a move. She'll go to that place, if that's what she's doing.'

'And so?' said Clarissa.

'We need to be in there.'

Clarissa looked at Kirsten. 'What? It's daytime. How are we going to walk in there in the daytime?'

'We can walk in there in the daytime,' said Kirsten. 'You'll have to be nimble enough.'

'You're not taking me in there during the day. It was bad enough last time. You chewed me out because I clocked someone with a kitchen implement.'

'Seoras said we had to accelerate this. We've got Hope lying in the hospital. They're not going to stop coming for you. We need to end this. This is a risk worth taking.'

'I agree,' said Perry.

'You're not the one going in,' Clarissa said to Perry. 'I'm constantly told I'm not spy material, not good at running around, and yet I'm going in.'

'I need you in there,' said Kirsten. 'I'll protect you. If we get found out, then we get found out. The time for waiting around is over. Your Chief Constable's lying in a hospital in a critical condition. Who knows what state Hope's in? We need to end this.'

Kirsten walked over to Clarissa and put her hand on her shoulder. 'We're going. Suit up!'

'You want me to put the black stuff on again?'

Kirsten went round to the boot and opened it up. 'No, this one.' She threw out some greyish clothing. It had patches of black, white and grey in it. 'This is urban cover,' she said, 'and also the balaclava, full mask, this time.'

'It doesn't do my hair any good.'

'Perry, you watch again. Advise us.'

It took about twenty minutes before Kirsten had Clarissa entering by the back gate onto the estate. She kept close to Clarissa, coaxing her forward as they approached the house.

'The good thing about daytime,' said Kirsten in Clarissa's ear, 'is that doors are open. But you've got to be very careful. You've got to keep yourself out of sight at all times. You watch carefully. Like now, how that servant is coming out and walking round the house. Well, he's actually a guard because he's done that twice already. He'll not be back for another minute. Let's go.'

Kirsten reached down, grabbed Clarissa's hand, and dragged her up out of their hiding position. Clarissa was in a whirl. She didn't know what was going on. All she knew was she had to keep following Kirsten.

Kirsten entered the rear of the house, ran down through a couple of corridors, and then found a room that led down to a cellar. She plonked Clarissa into the cellar, right into the far corner in the dark.

'You stay there. I will come and get you when I know where she's going.'

Clarissa spent the next hour in the dark. Every now and again, she would hear the creak of the house. There would be footsteps, and she'd wonder if someone was coming for her. Several times, she thought of Hope and then of Frank. How lucky he'd been, by comparison.

'Come on, old girl,' she said to herself. 'You need to man up for this. You need to make sure that you don't let anyone down.'

And then she heard the door of the cellar open. It closed, and she heard footsteps coming down. Clarissa stood up and looked around in the darkness. She could make out a small crowbar. Picking it up, she stole across to where the stairs came down, standing a few inches away. She heard the footsteps come down one, then two, then another couple of steps. Finally, they would be reaching the cellar. Clarissa picked the crowbar up, and swung it.

Kirsten stopped the crowbar, twisted it so that Clarissa let go, and then marched back with it across the room and put it where it had been.

She came back to Clarissa and, in hushed tones, said, 'You didn't even check who it was. You could have battered me. You could have been stuck with me unconscious and you having to get us out of here. When I say stay put, stay put. Your biggest problem is you do not listen. You just go off on one.'

'Kirstie, shut up,' said Clarissa bluntly, but in a quiet voice.

'I'm out of my depth here. I am scared witless, and you left me in the dark. Why?'

'Because Lady Cockburn's gone to bed? But prior to that, she did go to her secret room. I know where it is, and we're going in. That is why I did it. Once in a while, trust me. Now come on.'

Kirsten turned and crept up the stairs, Clarissa following behind her slowly. At the top, Kirsten opened the door, checked the corridor, and then pulled Clarissa out with her. They ran round the lower level of the house before getting up to the stairs. On the top floor, they had to hide round one corner while a maid busied herself cleaning. Once she'd stepped out of the way, Kirsten took Clarissa directly into what was a small library.

'So what, she just pull a book or something?'

'There's a hatch.'

'Oh,' said Clarissa.

'Quite clever really,' said Kirsten, and walked over to a wall section. She pushed it hard in one corner. The wall sprang back out, and the pair entered a corridor leading through to an office. There were no lights inside until Kirsten flicked a switch, and she let Clarissa go in first, before closing the door behind her.

'Well, here you are. I've got you in. Get to it.'

Clarissa looked at the room. Here and there were lots of Forseti symbols. There was a sacrificial dagger up on a shelf. Clarissa picked it up and turned it over.

'This is the same as the one they use. This must be hers,' said Clarissa. She looked over and saw a computer but it was bizarre, because it looked so old.

'Do you remember these?' she said to Kirsten.

'No,' said Kirsten. 'I don't remember them. I know what it is, though.'

'I remember working on these back in the day. One of the first ones. Why on earth does she have this here?'

'No internet. No connection. Old school. Most people would struggle to know what inputs or commands to put in it to get anything back. Probably got a database on it.'

'What?' said Clarissa. 'You mean she's seriously running this to keep all her information on?'

'Yes, that'll be exactly what she's doing. Hang on a minute,' said Kirsten, but Clarissa had already switched on the machine. There was a bip that came from the screen, but Kirsten was running her eyes everywhere, and then suddenly dived forward and pulled the plug on something else.

'You trying to kill us, Clarissa?'

'What do you mean, Kirstie? I'm switching on the machine. You said she could have a database on this. I'm going to have a look.'

'And you never checked what came out of the back of it.'

'What?'

'There's a fire switch attached to that computer. It's old school. Basically, you switch on the power, and it activates, unless you've pulled the plug.'

'What do you mean?' said Clarissa.

'This room goes up in flames. It would have done if I hadn't pulled that plug. That plug's attached to a device that just had its safety knocked off. It goes off as soon as you switch on that computer.'

'Am I okay now?' said Clarissa.

'See what you can find.'

Clarissa operated the computer like it was yesterday. It had been one of the first types she'd ever worked on and she pulled up a couple of databases that Lady Cockburn had stored on it.

'Find anything?' said Kirsten.

'Yes. Look at this. Sacrifice. It's a list of sacrifices. They actually kill people. They actually sacrifice people. Real people.'

'Like to Forseti?'

'Basically. Either that or it's the people who have stepped out of line. We've got a couple of people listed here, though.'

'Take a photograph of it. Take a photograph of everything that comes up on there. And keep going through it. Don't dally.'

'But we're fine. She's asleep. We're here.'

'We are stuck in a dead end,' said Kirsten. 'If somebody comes in here, where do I run? Nowhere. If somebody comes in here, I am shooting my way out. That changes everything. Therefore, we get in here, we do it quick, we get out.'

Clarissa put her head back down to the computer, then noticed that Kirsten had gone over and touched the sacrificial knife.

'It's quite an item isn't it?' she said.

'It is quite an item, and it was placed on a different angle up here than what you left it,' said Kirsten.

Clarissa waved her hand at her. 'Busy working,' she said. It took another twenty minutes of going through the computer before Clarissa had photographed everything on it.

'There's not much on it, not much at all. I'll close it back down,' she said. She did so and watched as Kirsten plugged the fire switch back in.

'At least that was useful,' said Clarissa. 'What do we do with it now?'

'We do nothing. We get out of here, we get back to the safe house, and then we decide our next move with everybody else. Don't think about what's going to happen next. We think about getting out of here, because if we don't, it changes everything.'

Kirsten took Clarissa up to the door, listened carefully, and then opened it. They stepped back into the library.

'Straight out,' said Kirsten. 'Straight out! Follow me. Don't say anything!'

Ten minutes later, they'd arrived back with Perry.

'Good timing,' he said. 'Did you get anything?'

'Yes,' said Kirsten. 'Good call. Very good call. You're quite a genius.'

Perry gave a smile, but it then turned back into more of a frown. 'We've had news from the hospital. It's not good. They're assessing Hope at the moment. She's not on life support, but she's on a lot of support. They're worried about the little one. Susan's still there. The other news is that the big boss and Anna have finally got out. They want to meet back at the house.'

'Good,' said Kirsten. 'Come on, let's go.'

She walked back to the car that Clarissa had arrived with her in, while Perry headed back on his own. As they sat in the car, with Kirsten driving, the air was frosty between them.

'What exactly is your problem with me?' Clarissa said to Kirsten.

'My problem is that in what I do, I have to be exact. I can't just go off on a tangent. You charge around like a bull in a China shop. Don't get me wrong, you're good at what you do. This art stuff, you see connections at times. You're good, really good. But you are a nightmare for someone like me.'

'That's probably why Seoras put me with you. Keep you on

your toes,' said Clarissa.

'And that bothers me as well,' said Kirsten.

'What? You don't like a bit of banter?'

'No. That you're terrified inside, and you put this front up, that everything's okay, and you can handle it. In my job, I need to know how people are, not how they want people to think they are.'

'Well, this is an old girl you will not teach new tricks to,' said Clarissa. 'Sometimes in your life, you've just got to front up and get on with it. That's what I'm doing, and trust me, I'm terrified to the core.'

Chapter 19

'Seoras, calm down.' Kirsten stood looking at him, her gaze never wavering.

'Calm down? They've taken out Jim. They've now beaten Hope to a pulp. Who knows how she is? They might have taken the little one with her. And you're telling me to calm down. We need to get these people now. We need to—'

'Calm down,' said Kirsten. 'You can't change what's happened. Hope's getting the best treatment possible.'

'And what's to stop them going in there again? What's to stop them going for her in the hospital?'

'Well, Susan's down there for a start,' said Perry.

'And you think Susan will stop them?'

'Susan has friends,' said Anna, quietly from the corner.

'What's that meant to mean?' said Clarissa.

'It means our friends have opted to get more friends to help Susan out,' said Perry. 'You probably don't want to hear this, Seoras, but they're right. Calm down.'

'We don't need to be calm,' blurted Clarissa. 'We need to get in there. Seoras is right. We need to go for them. We need to—'

'Don't be an idiot,' said Anna, her tone flat and level. 'You're not bringing anything to the situation, reacting like that. At the moment, we do need to do something. We need to act quickly. But foremost, we need to get our heads together and decide upon the plan of action, then go do it. Jumping around like this doesn't help anyone.'

'Have you got no feeling at all? That's our colleague out there. That's our friend. That's our Hope. And her wee one.'

'Clarissa,' said Sabine. 'They're right. Perry's right.'

'You can't just all sit like this, acting as if it's okay,' Clarissa retorted.

'Nobody said it was okay,' spat Sabine. 'None of us are sitting here saying it's okay, but we need to know how to react. We need to know where to go, how to bring this to a sensible solution. We've taken risks. It was said earlier on that we've taken risks. Both of you got inside houses and were trapped while you were discovering something. If you had been walked in on, then you may not have got out, and if you did, everything would have been blown.

'Obviously, this Forseti group is coming after us, whether we like it or not. We need to get this right, first time, so we don't have other colleagues in the hospital. You need to do this the right way,' said Sabine, walking over to Clarissa and putting her hand on her shoulder. 'For Pats.'

Clarissa raised her hand up to Sabine. 'For Pats, for Hope, for Jim.'

'I contacted Emmett,' said Perry. 'Looked at those addresses you got, names for sacrifices, to see what we can find out about them. Told Ross he has to be extremely quiet with it.'

'Good,' said Macleod. 'Emmett needs to hold the fort back at the station. He can do that with Ross.'

'So what is our play?' asked Sabine. 'Where do we go from

here?'

'Well, we know that they've got a Forseti circle at Loch Badanloch. Why, we don't know. We know why the other one was made at Loch Lee, to get the Revenge group in. This other one must be the real thing. The receipts show items were transported up there,' said Macleod.

'I looked at them,' said Perry. 'You're talking about proper lorries taking rocks. Things that need to carry weight, masonry. The last one was done by a removals firm, when it was plastic.'

'So, we need to get in there. If we could get in there,' said Clarissa, 'and find the circle, couldn't we charge them?'

'I'm not sure this is going to end with people being charged,' said Anna.

'We're not going down that route,' said Macleod. 'We will arrest them. We will find them and we will bring them in.' He saw Kirsten looking over at him. Her eyes said it wouldn't end that way but Macleod was convinced he had to. 'If we just take them out, I'm no better than them.'

'Seoras, I think this has gone beyond what you are,' said Kirsten.

'What we are is what we are. It's everything. We can't just walk around becoming the Forseti group, taking people out. We're not the Service,' said Macleod.

'Maybe this is more about self-preservation,' said Anna.

'What do you mean by that?' asked Macleod.

'You know what I mean by it,' said Anna. 'Three people in the hospital from your team, including your Chief Constable. You're lucky none of them are dead.'

'Well, I wanted to give this to you. I said you should go after it,' spat Macleod.

'And I would, but I don't have the people I can trust. I don't know where the leaks are in my organisation. That's why I'm here. That's why Kirsten's here. Because she doesn't work for me. You know you can trust her. I know I can trust her,' said Anna.

'But you're happy for us to investigate,' said Macleod, 'and we've got leaks. Look at Jim. You said you would protect our people. Where were your people last night with Hope?'

'Exactly,' roared Anna. 'I can't trust them. I've sent the last few I know I can trust to go with her now. You don't understand what happened to the Service. Kirsten does,' said Anna. 'It's taking time to build it back up. It's taking time to—'

'I'm sick of the excuses,' said Macleod, almost in a rage now.

'He's right,' said Clarissa. 'You said you would protect—'

'I protected your Frank. Don't forget that,' said Anna.

'Can I just step in here?' said Perry suddenly, walking into the middle of the room. 'Emotions are very high. I get it. I carried three babies out of a bomb blast, so I get it. My boss is currently fighting to save her child, so I get it. My friend Patterson is currently injured, so I get it. Our Chief constable is struggling, critical, so I get it. All of us in this room are suffering. All of us have got to go to places we don't want to go, especially as police officers. We're doing stuff here that we shouldn't be doing. But we need to focus on what we're asked to do.'

'Which was?' said Sabine.

'Find out who these people are. Foremost, we need to know who they are.'

'I think we've got a unique opportunity coming up,' said Anna.

'I think you're right,' said Perry.

'Explain,' said Clarissa.

'They've got a circle, here in the highlands. As I understand it, this is where they act. This is where they come together when they take their critical decisions—when they do a change, when they execute people. This is a place for them all to come together. Is that right?' He looked at Clarissa.

'It would seem to be,' she said. 'It's the ring. That's what the Revenge group thought, wasn't it?'

'They thought they were going to all the leaders,' said Sabine.

'We have a list of what they call sacrifices. We need to follow the sacrifice; we need to tail them and go to that meeting, not storm in now,' said Perry. 'Our link in at the moment is Lady Cockburn and Varney. I don't think Varney is necessarily at the head of the group, but Lady Cockburn is. She will not disappear anywhere, but on the other hand, until she goes to somewhere, we can't get any more out of her. The sacrifice though, we know, will be attending at some point.'

'But which one do we go for?' said Macleod.

'Top of the list,' said Sabine. 'You make a list. You take the one at the top. It's obvious. It's the way they think, isn't it? We can't follow all of them.'

'There were dates. Well, months anyway. This sacrifice was in this month. If she's still here, well then, sacrifice is still to happen,' said Perry.

Macleod suddenly reached to his pocket. He picked up a phone that wasn't his usual one, and the room fell silent.

'Seoras, it's Susan.'

'What's up?' asked Macleod.

'They've taken her into theatre. They've said it's for her, not for the baby at the moment. Whatever's happened inside, they're having to repair. They think she's got some internal bleeding.'

'Is it . . . ?'

'They're not saying. They don't know till they go in. She's going to be in the theatre for a while.'

'I want to come and visit her,' said Macleod. 'But I can't.'

'She's safe in this hospital. I've met some of our friends. Nobody will get to her here.'

'Keep me updated,' said Macleod.

'I doubt I'll hear anything for a few hours. Six to eight hours.'

'Okay,' said Macleod. 'Take care of yourself.' He switched off the phone and put it away in his pocket, knowing he'd have to get rid of the SIM card.

'How is she?' asked Perry.

'Taking Hope in for surgery. They think she might have an internal bleed. It's her they're worried about, not the wee one.'

Macleod felt the tears welling up in his eyes. He couldn't lose her. Not Hope. This wasn't what needed to happen. He wanted Jane, wanted to talk to her and pour his heart out. He couldn't be like that in front of the team. Macleod was the boss. He was the man who had to take charge, had to be the strong one in front of them. He felt a pair of arms slip around him. Kirsten was hugging him tight.

Clarissa got up too. Soon, they were all embracing each other. He saw the tears in Clarissa's eyes. Sabine was choking them back. Perry was as sombre as he'd ever seen him.

'We can't do anything for her,' said Macleod suddenly. 'Perry's right, as is Anna. We follow the sacrifice, but we do it well. This might be the one chance at this. We see where it takes us. If we get them all together, we arrest them, we do what we have to do, we make it work somehow. Make it so these people are no longer a viable threat to the public, to ourselves. Hopefully, that's behind bars.'

'Good,' said Anna. 'First plan then?'

'I'll get details,' said Perry. 'I'll talk with Kirsten. Make up a plan.'

'It's me, Clarissa, and Perry. We'll do the initial work,' said Kirsten. 'Anna, you have a second team ready, in case we have a split.'

'Good,' said Macleod. 'Get to it.'

He left the room and disappeared upstairs. When he got to the bedroom, he closed the door behind him. Getting down on his knees, he tried to pray, but there were no words. God knew what he wanted. God didn't need to be told. He heard a light knock at the door. Sniffing, he advised whoever it was to come in. He was still on his knees as the door opened, and Anna Hunt entered the room. Rather than get down beside him, she sat on the bed in front of him.

'They always said you were a religious man, but I'd never seen it until now. None of the rest of them will come up to you. You know that, don't you?'

'It's what it is to be at the top,' said Macleod. 'Yes, they'll hug you down there. But when you're off on your own, your own thoughts, your own ways, none of them will come to me, except Hope.'

'She's different, isn't she? I see that. Even Kirsten. Kirsten's not—'

'Kirsten's not Hope,' said Macleod. 'Kirsten is like the daughter I've never had. I care a lot for her, but she rails at me like I'm the father who got it wrong. Like a teenager. Can't see my side of it.' He gave a laugh. 'But Hope. Hope can see where I come from. Hope can feel it. She's a very special person to me,' he said. 'Only Jane trumps her.'

'Not by a lot either, though, is it?' said Anna. Macleod looked up at her. She smiled back. 'There was a man who ran the Service, who I could speak to, who I could get hold of. We were similar.'

'In what way?' asked Macleod.

'Saw things from a similar angle. We could talk about things openly. He shared little with other people, but he shared with me. In the end, the Service took him away from me.'

'I hope this doesn't take her away from me. I used to think if Jane hadn't had come along, if I was twenty years younger.'

'You don't go there,' said Anna. 'Don't go there.' And then she became very serious. 'You've had the benefit of her with you. I hope you get to see more of it.' She put her hand on Macleod's shoulder and went to leave, but he grabbed her hand.

'What?' he said. 'What happened to him?'

'Good old perceptive Macleod,' said Anna. 'I had to put a bullet in him. He destroyed the Service. I had to stop him.' She went to leave, but Macleod held her. 'I'm sorry,' he said.

He'd never seen Anna cry, but the tears flowed. 'I couldn't tell anyone. Only Kirsten knows, and I couldn't talk to her like this.'

For the next two minutes, Anna cried and sniffed, before standing up, smoothing down her clothes and wiping the tears from her eyes.

'Don't be too long, Seoras,' she said. 'They need you out there. I need you. We need to end this.' She gave a faint smile and left the room.

Chapter 20

Perry sat in the car and felt like this was his life now. He seemed to be the man watching people, and yet he felt he had done far better when he was out, engaging. He remembered Garve, pretending to faint from dehydration, and the information he'd got there. Part of him wondered if the life of a spy would suit him.

He reckoned he had the skills, the ability to learn many more of them, and an eye for deceit. But he also wondered would it suit him having to put people down, having to shoot people sometimes, not just simply arrest them? He wasn't sure that was him.

He thought Kirsten was magnificent in how she could conduct herself, in how she fought, in her attitude toward things. But it scared him that the same woman could put a bullet in someone and move on. That wasn't Perry.

He was currently sitting outside the flat of a young twenty-year-old woman called Chapel McKinley. She was the next one on the sacrifice list and, so far, had been to the supermarket to pick up a few groceries.

Also sitting in the car was Kirsten, with Clarissa in the rear. Clarissa demanded the rear so she could put her feet up and stretch out a bit. Perry thought she wasn't suited to stakeouts. Every five minutes she would start talking about something or other. So much so that Perry thought about buying a magazine and throwing it into the back seat. It was clearly bothering Kirsten as well, but not as much as when Clarissa called her Kirstie.

'Does this woman not do anything?' moaned Clarissa.

'She's got a little less bee in her bonnet than you,' said Kirsten. 'Would you just sit at peace?'

'Kirstie, you're talking to a dynamic detective here. On the arts team, we sort things out. We actually get on top of stuff quickly.'

Underneath it all, Perry thought they're just frightfully afraid, especially about Hope. He didn't blame them. He was worried too, for they'd heard nothing more. Everybody was also running on empty in terms of energy. Most had been up through the night. This would not stop though, and Perry reckoned that they'd be lucky to see another night's sleep within the next two or three. Especially as it was close to the end of the month and Chapel's date as a sacrifice had to be in his month.

'Should I pop out and get some more food?' asked Clarissa.

'You could just pop out and we'll leave you somewhere,' said Kirsten.

'There's no need for that sarcasm. I've told you before and—'

'I wish for five minutes you would just shut up,' said Kirsten. Perry glanced over at her. It was the first time he'd seen her truly snap. He was about to say something when he saw the door of the flat open.

'Heads-up! Looks like we require action, Clarissa, at last. Our girl's on the move.'

The young woman stepped out of the house. She had white hair, which made her highly conspicuous in a crowd, yet she was also thin and long, even though she wasn't as tall as Hope. She would reach up to Perry, but unlike his wide girth, this woman was thin without looking scrawny. Perry wished he could do that.

Chapel was dressed in a colourful skirt, with long boots underneath, with a rain jacket on top. She had a bag over one shoulder, and was now marching off into town.

'At least twenty yards behind me,' said Kirsten, and got out of the car. Perry watched as she walked off down the street. Twenty seconds later, Clarissa got out, and followed. Perry started the car up, and waited to be told to get on the move.

It was five minutes later, when he was advised they were in a shopping centre in town. He drove and parked up there. Getting out, he made it onto the central concourse and could see Kirsten at the far end.

She was standing outside one of the coffee shops, but across from it, looking into a mobile phone shop, apparently looking at the best deals. But a glance over her shoulder every now and again told Perry she knew where Chapel was.

Perry sat down on a bench in the middle of the concourse. He wouldn't be required, unless things went south. Clarissa passed the coffee shop once, then twice, and then a third time before Chapel McKinley got on her feet again. She walked along and passed a card stand sitting outside a shop. Perry was closest to her now and thought she'd glanced down before walking past.

He saw Kirsten follow her shortly after. Clarissa then met Chapel, coming back the other way. Chapel went past the card stand once again, and Perry thought the head flipped round to have a look.

He touched his earpiece and spoke to the team. 'I reckon she's looking at that card stand,' said Perry.

'Stay there, on it. Watch who goes by it. See if you can spot anything,' said Kirsten.

Perry sat back, almost whistling to himself, as he saw a few people come up and look at cards. Then he saw a man pass it. The man was then standing some twenty feet away, looking back at it as Chapel appeared. She picked up something from the stand, and Perry went to his earpiece.

'She's picked up something. Man across from the stand, twenty yards away, watching. Grey trousers, green shirt, blue jacket.'

'I see him! I've got our girl,' said Kirsten. 'Clarissa, pick him up. Perry, don't move at the moment.'

Perry saw Chapel moving away, clearly having something in her bag. Kirsten followed, and the man moved past Perry with Clarissa behind him. Perry saw the man look over his shoulder.

'You've been made, Clarissa,' said Perry quietly into his earpiece. He watched as the man furtively moved inside one store. Clarissa followed.

'Go with her,' said Kirsten.

Perry could hear Kirsten call for backup over the radio, wanting somebody else to pick up Chapel. As he did so, he entered the store and saw the man in the distance. Clearly, he could see Clarissa after him. She hadn't broken into a run though, and they were both oblivious to the shoppers as he ducked this way and that way past a range of clothing. He was nimble on his feet and Perry saw him come to a door. Going through it, he saw Clarissa follow shortly. When she got there, she tapped her earpiece and spoke to Perry.

'There are two ways here. I can't see him. I'm going right. You go left when you come through.'

Perry speeded up. He got through the door, looked to the right, but Clarissa was already down the corridor that was there. So, he turned left. He marched along, turned down another corridor and then came to the end of the passage. There was a room at the end where a woman was taking a mince pie out of a microwave.

'Can I help you?' she said.

'Sorry,' said Perry. 'I got lost. Where the heck's the shop?'

'Back that way. Just go through the door, all right?'

Perry nodded and turned, but it appeared he was out of the chase.

* * *

Clarissa still had eyes on the man, but he'd gone through the rear of the store, had come out, and had now gone into a department store that had all sorts in it. There were two floors, and Clarissa followed him across, past a section of books. From there, he went through the women's underwear section before arriving in men's clothing. It looked like he would duck through into the changing rooms, but at the last minute he peeled away.

'Where are you?' spoke Kirsten's voice in Clarissa's ear.

'In the department store. Ground floor,' said Clarissa.

'Stay on him. We're on our way.'

Clarissa saw the man stride through the section and then realised he was heading upstairs. He got on the lift, and she ran up the stairs, picking him up just as he came out of the lift. He clocked her again, and this time paced across the department store.

Heading through soft furnishings, passing by curtains and bed sheets, Clarissa saw the man head into the hardware section, with rows of pots and pans beyond. Looking beyond that, she saw the exit on the first floor. If he got through there, he could cut left, head down across the bridge and into the car park and away. Clarissa tapped her earpiece.

'Top floor. Are you able to cut off?'

'We're on the ground floor,' said Kirsten.

'Kirsten, he's gone upstairs. I'm just about to go into the cookware section. If he gets out there, he'll get away.'

'We're on our way, maintain pursuit, keep him in sight.'

Clarissa saw the man cut through the crockery shelves and instead of following him, she crouched down and disappeared behind a rack of saucepans. She wondered if he'd make a bolt for it. If he couldn't see her, maybe he'd panic, think she was close and run. If he did, he'd have to run up the aisle at the far side. It was a quiet part of the department store.

Clarissa, crouching quickly, sprinted as fast as she could, maintaining a low level until she got right up to the aisle she believed he would use. Beside her on the display was a cast iron frying pan. She picked it up and knelt down, waiting, wondering if someone would come round the corner. They would surely look at her and wonder what she was doing. Or would her quarry come to her?

She could hear steps. They were quick and then they stopped. *Was he wondering if the entrance was clear? Could he make it? Is that what was on?* She looked around, but there was nobody else about.

Then she heard the sprinting feet clipping along. They were

closer, definitely closer. *That must be him at the end.* Clarissa stood up as the man came to the end of the aisle. She caught him full and square in the face with the frying pan and he dropped to the floor.

She looked around quickly, putting the pan down on the display again. There was blood seeping out of the man's nose but he was out cold. She reached down and pulled him back into the aisle.

'Status.' It was Kirsten. What should she say?

'I have him,' said Clarissa.

'You what?' said Kirsten.

'I have him. Apprehended.'

'How? How have you apprehended him? You haven't put him in cuffs, have you? That's not going to work for an extraction.'

'He's not in cuffs. He's unconscious.'

'Where are you?' said Kirsten quickly.

'Saucers and pans, the cookware section upstairs.'

Clarissa looked around and then saw two figures hurrying through the store. They weren't running. They were going about as fast as they could without being noticeable. One was Kirsten. The other was Anna Hunt. Kirsten approached quickly, arrived at the end of the aisle, turned and looked down at the figure on the floor.

'What on earth?' she said. 'You were meant to follow him. We can apprehend him quickly, quietly. Take him when he's somewhere private. Not in the middle of a department store.' Kirsten looked around. 'Up there,' she said. 'That's a camera. They'd have clocked you smacking him in the face. I take it the reason his face is bloody is that you panned him.'

Anna Hunt arrived from behind. Kirsten went on to the

earpiece. 'Perry, where are you?'

'In the department store. Just heading up to the first floor.'

'Clarissa is going to meet you at the exit. Get her out of here quick. Back to the car. Wait for my instruction.'

'Walk that way,' Kirsten snarled at Clarissa. Clarissa gave Kirsten a sharp look, but then walked over towards the entrance, where Perry joined her and led her off to the car.

'Got to get him out,' said Anna, 'with nobody being the wiser, and I need to do something about that CCTV.'

'Him first,' said Kirsten.

Together, the two women picked the man up, and while crouching low, they carried him down the aisles until they could find a staff entrance to the back of the shop. Anna opened it, and together they dragged the man through. Kirsten shoved him behind some boxes.

'You neutralise the CCTV,' Kirsten said to her. 'I'll get this guy out of here.'

About fifteen minutes later, Perry was sitting in the car park, along with Clarissa. He received instruction over the earpiece to go round to the back of the shopping centre and pull up beside one of the delivery points. As he got there, Perry noticed it was quiet at that one. No deliveries currently.

He was told to reverse the car up tight, and then pop the boot. He did so, and in his rearview mirror, he saw Anna and Kirsten throwing an unconscious man into the boot and closing it. They then clambered into the back.

'Right, Perry,' said Kirsten. 'Get us back to the safe house. And then I want you to go back to Chapel McKinley's and just see if she's there. Pick up the tail again. We've got some work to do with our colleague in the back.'

'We'll see what we can get out of him,' said Clarissa.

'You do not say a word,' said Kirsten.

'Kirstie, I got him.'

'I swear, you call me Kirstie again and I will get Perry to stop here, and I'll put you down somewhere.'

'I think we can both learn from the example of Mr Perry here,' said Anna. 'Calm heads, people.'

Perry gave a little smile to himself. Maybe he could be a spy after all. It seemed he had the demeanour for it.

Chapter 21

Macleod was watching the man strapped to the chair in the middle of the lounge. The man was currently wearing a blindfold and could neither move his legs nor his arms. Despite this, sitting very close by was Kirsten. Macleod noted she never took her eyes off him.

Macleod had wondered whether it was best to have one or two people in the room. Tensions were running high, especially with Hope being in theatre. Macleod still wasn't sure how she was as Susan hadn't contacted him. Maybe there was no news. He knew it was playing on him, and if it was playing on him, it was playing on everyone. Well, except Anna Hunt, who looked calm as she began questioning the man.

The man was clearly afraid and stammered out answers to questions. He constantly avoided the root question of who he worked for, what he was doing with the drop, and what the drop had said. Anna continued in a cool voice.

Meanwhile, beside her, Clarissa was getting more and more agitated. In the unusual guise of black tracksuit bottoms and a black t-shirt, she was wandering round and round and clearly making Kirsten slightly annoyed. Perry was sitting in the other corner, watching carefully.

Macleod marvelled that considering all that was going on, Perry could still see the wood from the trees. He was still focused on what needed to be done. Not as cold as Anna, but certainly not missing the point of what needed to be found out. He understood why Anna had spoken about Perry possibly being good for the Service, although his fitness would have to change. Perry was also probably too kind at heart.

'And who gave you the money to make the drop?' said Anna, for the fourth time.

'Don't know. They just give us the money.'

'Where did you get your orders from?'

'An envelope dropped to me.'

'And how did this work the first time?' asked Anna. 'A random envelope appeared and said do this. You know that's how people get in trouble going through customs.'

'I needed the money. So I just did it.'

'Does the name Forseti mean anything to you?' asked Anna.

Macleod saw the man flinch. He knew he wasn't aware of it, being blindfolded but Macleod could tell quite easily, that he'd heard that name before.

'So, you do know Forseti?' said Anna. 'Does it scare you?'

It clearly did, as the man was trembling now. 'What was the message about?' asked Anna.

'I don't know,' said the man.

'How many people do you drop messages off to for them every month? On average,' said Anna, quietly.

'Three or four,' said the man.

'How often to this one?'

'I don't know who this one is. It's the point of the drop.'

'Did you stop the first time to check? Make sure they were there? Somebody would have checked. I bet it was you, wasn't it? You will not pass out this information to too many people. The first time they dropped it, they told you to stand and watch, didn't they? You see,' said Anna. 'I know how these things operate, and I don't think they operate very well with you guys. Bit of a quick drop. In an open area like that? She walked past it three times. Did you know that? Three times waiting for your drop. Were you late?'

'You'd think they would have perfected the hand switch,' said Kirsten.

'Ah, the hand switch,' said Anna, and then saw Macleod's bemused face. 'You walk one way, I walk the other, and as we cross, we just pass it on. In a crowd, no one none the wiser. But you guys didn't do that. You guys put it out in the open and left it. Anybody could have come along and picked that up. Anyone. You know what that means?'

The man dropped his head but didn't say anything.

'That means you're expendable. You'd only be that sloppy with expendable people,' said Anna. 'People they don't care about. So, if they get discovered, we just get rid of them. At the moment, I'm looking at a dead man!'

'Might not be a dead man if he helps us,' said Kirsten.

'He'll be a bloody dead man if he doesn't start talking,' said Clarissa suddenly.

Anna gave an annoyed look, and Kirsten turned and stared at Clarissa with a look of daggers. Anna simply raised her left hand, showing that Clarissa should stay quiet.

'We might be able to make a deal,' said Anna. 'You and I? We could probably get you away somewhere, get you out of here. You need to tell me, though. Tell me what's going on. Because at the moment, we're the only thing stopping you from being found out. We make a move on these people, they'll say it was you. When do you next have to check in?' asked Anna suddenly.

'Don't check in. Never check in,' said the man.

'How do they know if you're there or not? Do you tell them when you're going away?'

The man nodded.

'And?' said Anna.

'Meant to be away. Meant to be away tomorrow. Spain.'

'You could stay in Spain. Got a girlfriend? Wife? Mrs? Kids?'

'Girlfriend,' said the man. 'Going tomorrow.'

'What was in the package?'

'I don't open the package,' he said.

'You ever thought of having a peek?' asked Anna. 'Never thought that maybe you should have a peek. Just in case things went south like this and you could pass some information and get some help. Most couriers peek, you know that, if they can. That's why things are sealed properly, not just a sticky envelope. Or do they do that?' The man shook his head. 'And you never looked?'

The man went quiet again, and suddenly Clarissa stood up and stepped forward. She went to grab the man by the collar, but Kirsten blocked her.

'Kirstie, get out of my way. He's going to damn well tell us.'

'Clarissa,' said Macleod.

'He's sitting there, Seoras, just sitting there. He knows something. The swine knows something, I'm telling you that.' Clarissa lunged again and Kirsten was just too slow as Clarissa grabbed the man by the collar. She shook him in the chair. 'You damn well tell us, or you won't walk out of here. You tell us.'

Then Kirsten took Clarissa's wrists, applied a bit of pressure and moved Clarissa away.

'Well, that was said with passion,' said Anna. 'Maybe I should just let you go with this guy.'

The man was shaking his head and Macleod wondered if Kirsten had let Clarissa grab hold of him. Macleod could feel a vibration in his pocket and knew it was one of his phones. He excused himself and stepped out of the room.

'Seoras, it's Susan.'

'What's up?' asked Macleod. He could hear the emotion in Susan's voice. Choking, struggling to say what she was going to say.

'They've taken Hope into theatre again. It's an emergency C-section. They want to get the baby out. They're not happy, really not happy. Very worried. Worried about her too. I don't know where this is going, Seoras. I don't know where this is going.'

'It's okay,' said Macleod. 'Stay there. Stay with John. Be with him. Give him what support he needs. They need you at the moment, Susan, okay? I know how you're feeling, but they need you. There's no one else there. You've got to be the strong one. Talk to Anna's people. Make sure they know how to protect you all. If you see her,' said Macleod, 'give her my best.'

'I will,' said Susan, and then she ended the call. Macleod reeled for a moment. A C-section. Getting the baby out, could lose both of them. It wasn't good. They wouldn't have needed to do that except something must be seriously wrong.

He took a moment and breathed deeply, thinking of the red-haired woman he'd first met down in Glasgow, about to go on a first case with him. Macleod remembered how badly he'd thought of her. He remembered how proud he had become, thinking of her becoming a mum. Fighting to hold back tears, he didn't know if it was the lack of sleep or the whole emotion of what was going on. His frustration at not being able to get things done. Not being further on with this, having wrapped the case up, protected his people. But at the moment, he was struggling not to just burst.

However, he gripped his hands into fists, let the rage soak out, took a deep breath, and went back to do his job. As he opened the door, he could see Clarissa being restrained by Sabine. Anna was her calm self in the middle of the room. However, Kirsten looked agitated. Perry was also on his feet. It was unusual for him to intervene in any physical fashion. When he saw Macleod, he stepped across and whispered, 'Been a bit of a kerfuffle. I thought it was going to come to blows between Kirsten and Clarissa. Sabine stepped in.'

Macleod walked over to Anna and whispered in her ear, 'Where are we at?'

'We've just made a deal,' said Anna proudly. 'Our man here is going to disappear off to Spain. He's told us all he knows. Not that it's much. But he'll get out of the way for a while. We know that there's something happening tonight. I suggest the rest of us leave the room. Kirsten, you might want to babysit.' said Anna. Kirsten glared over, then looked back at Clarissa, who stomped out of the room, followed by Sabine.

Macleod turned to Perry. 'Go give Sabine a hand. Get the Rottweiler calmed down.'

When Perry had left, Anna indicated Macleod should follow her, and she went through into a different room.

'People get awfully upset. Creates bad judgment,' said Anna.

'Perry said she was going to go for Kirsten.'

'She went for Kirsten. She's very lucky that Kirsten has got superb control. Kirsten could have killed her without even thinking about it. Urquhart is very temperamental.'

'That she is,' said Macleod. 'But she's also quite brilliant at times. It's why I put up with her.'

'You put up with her because you need that side. It's not in you. You don't have that feisty nature,' said Anna. 'You surround yourself with people that fill the gaps. I do it too. You're talking to someone else who leads, Seoras. You don't need to be coy with me.'

Macleod took a deep breath. 'Where are we at?'

'We know that the sacrifice is going to be heading off soon, tonight, that much the man knew. He knew nothing else, and he basically surmised what he told me because he had to get the message out quick. That wasn't normal. Usually, you'd have a lot longer to arrange it, he said. That's why it was sloppy, but I think they're sloppy anyway.

'So we follow our sacrifice, see where they go, if it's the big meeting. I think it might be. If Cockburn's involved, and this is somebody coming into the circle to be killed or disposed of or whatever, then they could all be there. It's a perfect time for us to take them.'

Macleod nodded.

'I know you don't like this way of doing it. I know you're not happy. You're struggling to think, how do I get evidence? How do I put them behind bars? You may not get a chance, Seoras.'

Macleod looked at her, then turned away. 'I know,' he said. But then Anna walked over to him and put her hand on his shoulder.

'What is it?' said Anna.

'They've taken Hope in for an emergency C-section. Susan

doesn't know how bad or what's going to come of it.'

'I'm sorry,' said Anna. Macleod turned and Anna let him cry onto her shoulder. 'Let it out,' said Anna. 'I know what she means to you.'

When Macleod had calmed himself down again, Anna stood with him, her hands on his shoulders, and looked into his face. 'Don't tell the others,' she said.

'Why?' asked Macleod.

'You know why,' she said. 'Clarissa is above boiling point. She's ready to explode. I don't need a loose cannon, but I've got one. What I really don't need is a loose cannon who's got nothing left to hold back for. You'll also scare the rest of them. Even Kirsten.'

'Kirsten?'

'Do you think she's cold? She's not. Remember, when she first came into the force, she came with Hope and you. Yes. I think she idolises you in a lot of ways, but she does Hope too. Hope was someone she aspired to be, too. In fact, she took a lot of what Hope had, the calmness, the surety, the doggedness to find things out, the way to follow process, as opposed to the inspirational thought or that ability to read people that you have. We keep it between you and me until we get this done. Agreed?'

Macleod wearily nodded his head. 'And if you need me, Seoras, you tell me,' said Anna, 'because I need you. This night, or whatever follows.'

Chapter 22

Macleod managed to get some sleep in the afternoon of that day, but still had heard nothing back from Susan. If Anna had heard anything from her people, she wasn't letting Macleod know. He understood where she was coming from. They needed to be focused, and the idea that something had happened to Hope could send several of them over the edge. He had no news about Jim either. When he woke up that evening and came down to the kitchen, Perry was making soup.

'Feeling better for that?' said Perry.

'I'd like to say yes,' said Macleod, 'but I didn't sleep well.'

'Not easy to sleep during the day,' said Perry. 'And whatever else is bugging you.'

'I'm sorry,' said Macleod. Perry walked past him and shut the door of the kitchen before coming back to him.

'I know you're holding out on something. You and Anna disappeared into the room the other day. I heard you crying. It's obviously something bad. I don't need to know if you're needing to keep it quiet. If something has happened, some of the others might not take it that well.'

'Just, let's get on with it,' said Macleod.

'That's understood,' said Perry. 'Loud and clear. I take it you want soup. It's tomato, only cans they had in here.'

Macleod nodded, and then sat down to a bowl of soup beside Perry.

'Do you ever regret taking up this post? It was different down in Glasgow.'

'Regret? No,' said Perry. 'I can't regret it. I saved three babies doing this job. Three that may have been dead if it wasn't for me. That's what keeps me going. That and the other people that we've brought to justice. But this one's been rough. I won't lie to you, Seoras,' said Perry.

'Rough on us all. But you seem to keep your cool.'

'I don't think I have a button that says explode,' said Perry, reflectively. 'Seem to be someone that just takes it on the chin and thinks it through. I think too much sometimes and that's what frustrates people. I think it frustrates Tanya.'

'You saved her life,' said Macleod.

'I know,' said Perry. 'I asked her to come up here. Well, I didn't ask. I sort of hinted. And then she got the job with you. I got her all the way up here. And then, well . . .'

'What holds you back?' asked Macleod.

'Don't want to disappoint two people,' said Perry. 'I don't think I've ever had two women like me at the same time. Not properly like. You ever felt that?'

Macleod laughed. 'No,' he said. 'It's not happened to me.'

'I've put my life on the line for both of them,' said Perry, once again reflecting. 'I like Susan,' he said. 'But I don't know. I don't think it would work between the two of us long term. I've got a few years on her. Tanya. Well, we always got on. I also think that it would be okay working with Tanya. We wouldn't have to move our work because she isn't working with me directly. I would find it rough, I think, working with Susan if we were more than what we are now. Just partners. What do you think?' asked Perry.

'Do you know something, Perry? I've had Tanya come to me and ask me about you. I've had Susan come to me and ask me about you. You've now come to me and asked me about them. I think I should be left alone, Perry, because I've got other things on my plate that really need my attention.'

'Sorry,' said Perry. 'It's just—'

'Look, Perry, I'm not going to give you advice on women, because, frankly, I messed that up for so long. However, I will tell you, don't hang about. You don't know what happens, what can change. So decide what you're going to do, and do it.'

The two men sat, slurping their soup, until they'd finished. Perry took the dishes and washed them, while Macleod wandered in to find Anna Hunt sitting on the sofa. He wondered if she was asleep, but then he saw a smile.

'The waiting's the hardest part,' said Anna, 'especially when you're in charge.'

Macleod shook his shoulders. 'Need to be out there,' he said.

'Kirsten's got this. Got Sabine with her, and Clarissa in the car.'

'You put Clarissa out with Kirsten again?'

'Clarissa needed to do something. Clarissa can't hold her anger. She has to expunge it. It has to be put away somewhere. Kirsten will know that and can handle her. And besides, Sabine's there. She's a very competent young woman.'

Macleod had got to know Sabine through the Arts team and she certainly knew how to handle Clarissa. It was a good call by Anna, but she was right. Just waiting for something to happen was tough.

Macleod caught another couple of hours' sleep because there was nothing else to do. He was then awoken by Anna Hunt.

'They're on the move,' she said. 'Get yourself ready. Downstairs in five minutes—we'll get on the move too.'

'I guess this is it,' said Macleod.

'This is it,' said Anna. Five minutes later, he entered the living room and watched as Anna concealed two guns on her person and several knives.

'I hope it doesn't come to that,' he said, but she simply didn't look at him. Jumping into the car, Anna allowed Perry to drive, sitting in the front seat beside him, with Macleod in the rear.

'We'll be tailing a couple of miles back,' said Anna. 'I don't want two cars too close up behind. Apparently, Chapel McKinley is heading out to the northwest of Inverness.'

Anna sat watching her phone, occasionally giving Perry directions. The tone of the car was calm but intense. There was no getting away from the moment. This would be their chance if they'd decided correctly, if this was a proper meeting to bring someone in, someone at the top. After all, they had seen several branches cut off. Maybe they needed to build again. Macleod hoped so, hoped this would have the people they needed.

He asked Perry where they were going after a while, and Perry said Loch Badanloch was near.

Anna Hunt indicated they would pull up soon, and Perry took a small track off the road to find another car awaiting. Clarissa was there, along with Sabine, but Kirsten was gone.

'Where's Kirsten?' asked Macleod.

'Kirstie's on up ahead,' said Clarissa. 'She's staying close to the woman. We're following in behind. Here, she told us to give you these.'

Clarissa held in her hand several earpieces, and Macleod put one into his ear, as did Anna Hunt. Anna instantly tapped hers. Macleod could hear a tapping come back.

'She can't speak at the moment,' said Anna. 'Which direction did she head off in?' she asked Clarissa.

'It's up by the loch. You go that way.'

'Let's move then. Everybody stay tight, close and quiet. See anything, make sure you let us know. Either tap me on the shoulder, or you give a three-tap on the earpiece. Two taps back means you're clear to speak.'

Macleod looked at his motley crew, all dressed in black. Perry and Clarissa didn't suit tight black bottoms. In a tight top, Perry's frame was large and although he wasn't wholly unfit, he certainly was a size larger than he should have been. Clarissa just didn't look herself without a shawl. He wondered about himself, an old guy in young person's clothing. Anna Hunt, however, looked impressive. She wasn't that far off his age, was she? Well, maybe ten years. But she looked the part, and for that, he was thankful.

As they marched through the heather and the bogland, Anna led them up past the loch and off towards a stone building. It looked like a fallen down castle, for there were some turrets, but clearly it was in disrepair. Could it have been an old stately house, possibly? Looking at it, it seemed to be a ruin.

'She's up ahead. Kirsten's staying put now. We're going to join her,' said Anna quietly to everyone. 'Stay close to me. Don't speak.'

Rain had fallen, sending a chill through Macleod. It was just typical, feeling like winter, although it was summer. The rain was cool, and the dark night didn't help, putting Macleod on edge. As they got close, he saw Kirsten waving them on. He went to the front of the pack, along with Anna, and the three knelt down together.

'There's no security in place,' said Kirsten.

'That's not good, is it?' said Macleod. 'You'd think if they were bringing the head honcho, they'd—'

'You misunderstand,' said Kirsten. 'This is good.'

Clarissa had made her way up into the conversation now. 'No, Seoras. If they have got nobody here, it's because it's their most sacred rituals. There's the Forseti Circle, somewhere. It's a good thing there's no security.'

Kirsten indicated that everyone should be quiet, and moving off to the side, they followed her until she stopped in position and pointed. In the middle of the ruin, amidst torchlight, Macleod could see Chapel McKinley. She was getting undressed and changing into white robes. Across from her, slightly in shadow, Macleod thought he saw someone in a brown robe. They took Chapel's hand and led her away once she had dressed. Kirsten motioned everyone should stay put and disappeared into the dark.

Two minutes later, there was a tap on the earpiece. Anna tapped back.

'Follow me up. There's like a shed here. It looks like a groundskeeping shed or something. But it's large. They've taken Chapel inside it. In saying that, the doors are open on one side. I'm going up for a closer look,' said Kirsten. 'Come up to my point.'

Anna corralled her people up and they watched the barn with the open door. Kirsten peered out of it and indicated they should come forward. Together, they all crawled up to the barn, sat down on haunches and leaned inside.

'It's a Forseti circle,' said Clarissa incredibly quietly. 'It's full.

Look at them. It's full. There's ten. Ten plus the sacrifice.'

Macleod could see a circle lit by blazing torches. The circle did indeed have ten positions. These looked like actual stones though—not the fake ones they'd seen at Loch Lee.

At the head was one figure standing, dressed in a hooded red robe. He was speaking in a language Macleod didn't understand. He looked larger and stronger than the others, and he showed something with his speech. Suddenly, the circle broke into life. There were chants, and then the sacrifice, Chapel McKinley walked towards the middle, where there was the large stone. A stone similar, although real and not plastic, to the one that Bairstow had killed himself on. Macleod wondered if Chapel would be doing the same thing.

Chapter 23

Macleod was about to step forward, seeing that Chapel was heading towards the middle of the circle. He was worried she would take her life, but Anna clamped a hand on his shoulder.

'Wait,' she whispered. 'You don't know what's happening yet. We also need to corner these people.'

Macleod was edgy, but he held his position and watched as Chapel simply stood in the middle. There was a kerfuffle, however, towards the edges of the barn, and two of the figures, who had been seated, pulled another figure into the middle. These figures were wearing brown as well, except that the one in the middle wore a blue robe. One of the brown figures returned to their seat at the edge, but the other removed the hood of the blue figure. Macleod recognised Varney.

'This could be interesting,' said Anna in his ear.

Macleod watched the rather macabre tableau as Varney was dragged on to the middle stone and tied down to it. Macleod could feel the urge to get up. Whatever was happening to Varney, he didn't want it to happen. And given that the same positional stone had before been associated with death and sacrificial rites, it couldn't be good.

He went to creep forward again, but Anna's hand firmly locked on his shoulder.

'Stay put,' she said. 'You will not contain them all. We need to get ourselves sorted into a circle around them. We need to—'

But Macleod was looking into the circle. Chapel McKinley, in her white robe, was now standing behind the blue-robed Varney and Macleod could see her being handed what looked like a sacrificial knife. He felt Anna's hand, but Macleod pushed her arm away and charged forward.

'Police! Stand down! Police!'

Before he could reach the middle, Macleod saw Varney's throat being sliced by Chapel McKinley. The blood spattered onto her white robe, but she held her hand up with the knife, as if she'd just won a prize. However, the brown robes stood up, seeing Macleod run to the middle, several running towards him.

Behind him, Macleod could hear the shouts of Anna, telling the others to stand and grab whoever they could. Macleod ran forward and dived at Chapel McKinley. But she was a young woman and turned, using his weight to throw him past her to the ground. He looked up to see her knife raised, now coming towards him. There was a shot, and she spun one way, before a second shot spun her the other. Anna Hunt appeared beside him quickly.

'Get down and stay down, you idiot,' she said.

There were more shots. Macleod thought he heard somebody else going to the floor. He looked over and saw Perry, in hand-to-hand combat with somebody in brown. Perry was doing all right until the man head-butted him, causing Perry to stumble backwards.

The man looked like he was pulling out a weapon, but was suddenly clattered from the side, a large rock thrown at him from point-blank range. Clarissa stood over the man, shouting at him aggressively, diving on top of him and landing punch after punch.

It was all too crazy. It was all getting out of hand. The yells and the screams resonated around the inside of the barn. And then Macleod realised other people were firing guns, not just Anna and Kirsten.

He crawled along the ground to get behind a rock and then looked over to see Sabine pinned down, gunfire tracing around her. Seeing the man who was firing at her, Macleod wondered what to do. The man hadn't clocked Macleod, and he was now standing up to run towards Sabine.

Macleod picked himself up, ran forward and threw himself at the man. But the man was quick, and all Macleod could do was swing a left arm, catching the man's foot. It clattered into his other foot, and the man tumbled forward onto the ground. He rolled, however, getting himself back up, and Macleod saw the man looking for him, about to raise his weapon. Then he was hit from the side by Sabine. She kicked the man hard to the head, then she dived on him, raining down blows.

Macleod saw Kirsten, across the barn, throw somebody into the wall. He spun round looking, desperately, trying to understand what was going on in the melee. In the back of his mind, he realised he'd brought this about. Had Anna been right? It was too late to think about that now.

Macleod looked across the barn and saw the hood fall off one of the brown-robed figures. It was Lady Cockburn. She was running over towards the one who was dressed in red, who had been at the head of the ceremony when Macleod had entered the barn. It was clearly a man, given the shape of the figure, and she seemed to grab him, pushing him towards an exit. They were disappearing out into the dark.

Macleod looked to see if anyone was following them, but Anna Hunt was engaged with two other figures, and Kirsten was nowhere to be seen.

The dark of the shed didn't help, only exposed by flaming brands that cast shadows across the walls. Macleod picked himself up. They had to get the head, and the man in the red surely was the head. The meeting had been called. They were honouring Forseti, led by the figure in red, and Lady Cockburn was protecting them.

Macleod tore off after the red figure and then felt himself being tripped by somebody on the ground. He hit the ground hard, and someone jumped on him from behind. An arm went around his neck, and he felt himself being throttled. And then the arm went limp. The figure, however, was lying on top of him, and Macleod couldn't shake the weight. It seemed to roll off him, though, and Macleod turned round to see Clarissa standing there, a rock in her hand.

'The one in the red,' said Macleod. 'Through that door.'

Clarissa reached down and picked Macleod up. 'Go,' she said, 'go!'

The two of them ran off, out of the door, into the dark. His team was behind him, engaged in a battle, but Macleod had to get hold of this figurehead. Whoever the one in the red was, he needed to be found. Needed to be identified, at least.

'I can't see a thing now, in the dark.' Macleod turned round to see a blazing torch behind him.

It was Clarissa. 'You've got to have some way of seeing out here. It's pitch black,' she said.

Macleod pointed ahead. 'Over that direction. I think they've gone that way.'

There was a small path, like a deer path or sheep path, cut into the ground. Clarissa led the way, and the two ran forward. It bent this way and that, and they splashed through small puddles, the rain now beating down on them. As they legged it forward, Macleod couldn't see any figures. But then he stopped. Something had been there on the side. He'd passed something.

'Clarissa, come here. Bring the torch here.'

'Don't let them get away,' she said.

'They may already have,' said Macleod.

Clarissa turned round, and Macleod took the brand off her. He knelt it down close into the mire beside him and saw some sort of a manhole with a circular handle at the top.

'Open that,' he said, 'then stay back.'

Clarissa reached down, undid the manhole and pulled, lifting a metal lid on a hinge. She let it drop to one side, and Macleod looked inside. There was a lit tunnel. The light wasn't great, but it was enough. More like the emergency lighting, after a building has had its fire alarm sounded.

'You want to go down there?' said Clarissa. 'How do you know they've gone that way?'

'Did you see any cars?' asked Macleod.

'No,' said Clarissa.

'Then they must have gone somewhere. They must have come here from somewhere. Makes sense, to have a tunnel leading to it.'

He clambered onto a small ladder in the tunnel. 'Stick the brand,' he said, handing it to Clarissa, 'into the ground, so the others know where to follow to.'

Macleod clambered down the metal rungs and into a tunnel that was damp on the floor. It could accommodate two people wide. It was tall enough for him, although he thought Hope might have to crouch. *Hope*, he thought. Suddenly, she came back into his head. He prayed she was okay before he heard above him, Clarissa clambering down the metal rungs.

'Come on then,' she said. 'Let's go.'

'Careful,' he said. 'They may have guns. Some of them in there had guns.'

'I did spot that, Seoras,' said Clarissa. Together, the two ran along the tunnel. They were no sprinters, either of them, but they kept up as good a pace as they could. *Lady Cockburn is in her sixties. She couldn't keep up a good a pace like this either,* thought Macleod. And the person with her didn't look that sprightly. The tunnel curved this way, and that, descended at some points, and then climbed. Macleod could hear people up ahead, and he drove Clarissa on, telling her to keep going. His earpiece was activated with three taps, and he put two taps back.

'Situation in the barn's under control,' said Anna. 'Where are you?'

'There's a flaming brand. I'm in a tunnel, chasing our quarry. Lady Cockburn's got the guy in the red. I think that's how they got up to the barn. We're through this tunnel that's their escape. We're close,' said Macleod. He had to stop every now and again, trying to suck in his breath.

'You on your own?' asked Anna.

'Negative,' said Macleod. 'I've got Clarissa with me.'

There was silence for a moment, and then Anna Hunt said, 'We will join you. Perry and Sabine can take care of here.'

Macleod looked across at Clarissa as they realised they were the closest. Anna and Kirsten were well back, and yet they were armed. They were the people who could handle this. Macleod took a deep breath and continued to run hard.

They came to a bend in the tunnel, and at the far end, they could see some stepladders. Macleod saw a foot disappearing at the top of it. He ran closer.

Clarissa and he arrived at the stepladders and noted that the lid of the cover above them had been closed. Quickly, they ran up. Macleod went first up the ladder, opened the manhole, and threw it open. He stepped out, but as he did so, realised that this could be the stupidest thing he'd done.

He threw his hands up as a foot tried to kick him. It wasn't a strong foot. It wasn't like Kirsten or Anna would have done. They would have knocked him into the middle of next week. This one, however, knocked him to one side, and for a moment, he was temporarily stunned. Then he saw the red figure, led by Lady Cockburn, disappearing into the hedges in front of him. He fought and hauled himself up, dragging himself out through the manhole cover but keeping low. Clarissa followed, charging out like a wild bull.

'They went into those hedges,' said Macleod

'Hedges?' said Clarissa. She looked around her. In the distance, Macleod could see a building with lights, but Clarissa was watching carefully everything around her. 'I know this place,' she said. 'This estate. That's one of their buildings. This is the . . . Seoras, this is their maze.'

'It's their what?' blurted Macleod.

'It's their maze. They've got a hedge maze at the back of their summer house.'

Macleod looked over at the lights coming from the house, which seemed to be a lot bigger than any summer house he'd ever seen.

'That's just like a whole other building,' he said.

'Well, it's the summer house, but yes, it's probably where they got everyone else to meet. That's where the cars will be.'

'Well, maybe we could run round the maze, hold them in,' said Macleod.

'Not from here we won't,' said Clarissa. 'This is the encompassed bit. This is the middle of it.'

She turned and looked down at the manhole that had been opened up. 'This is covered up normally. This is the centre of the maze, look.'

Macleod realised that part of the manhole cover had something slid back off it, that would have prevented the manhole cover being seen. 'We'll have to follow them into the maze,' he said.

Clarissa looked at him. 'Shouldn't we wait for the other two?'

'It could be a while,' said Macleod. 'There's no option.'

He suddenly thought of the team. Clarissa and he were possibly the two worst people to be on foot pursuing. But that's what it was. It would come down to this. He took a deep breath. 'Come on, Rottweiler,' he said to Clarissa. 'Let's do this.'

Chapter 24

Macleod could feel the sweat on his brow as he entered the deadly maze. It was incredibly dark and making out where the hedges were in front of him was a game in itself. Slowly he walked along, Clarissa behind him, and peered round the corner of one of the hedges. He could see no one and so continued. As he walked along, he halted and turned to Clarissa.

'You know this maze,' he whispered. 'How big is it?'

'I know people who have got lost in it for three hours.' Macleod stared at her. 'It's big, Seoras. It's a significant maze. And it's not one of those with one route. It goes everywhere.'

Macleod was very conscious that he didn't have a weapon. All his life, he'd never carried a gun. He was a police officer. That's not what they did. They had special units for that. If guns were required, the special unit would attend. Macleod solved murders. He put his feet on the ground and sought clues. He went through files, went through information, and he found a killer. And then he arrested them.

This, he thought, would not end up in court. But if it did, it would probably be himself in the dock. Hauled up for malpractice, or whatever else you wanted to call it. He edged further along the hedge, his hand running along the side, touching twigs as he went. He continued, slowly, wondering exactly where the others were. Did they know the hedge ahead?

Then Macleod thought, *maybe this is a different sort of game. After all, Lady Cockburn has been unmasked. They are heading back to their building. What could they do now? Will she give herself up? To get the red-robed figure away? Whoever he is, there is no doubt of her involvement. She must realise that we know, must realise that the Forseti group will have to burn her arm of the operation. Indeed, they might have to burn most of the operation, except for the person at the top.*

So what will they do now? Where will they run? Will they get out of the maze quickly? Lady Cockburn's only option is to kill anybody else who is in her arm of the operation. She would have to put them all down and hope that they were operating on their own. There's no guarantees they were.

Macleod was fifteen minutes wandering around hedges, before he realised Clarissa was no longer behind him. He didn't know if he'd moved too quick, she'd moved too slow, or if she'd just gone off on her own. He listened, though, and he could hear Lady Cockburn whispering to the other figure. 'This way,' she said. 'The others can take care of them.'

This way? Others? thought Macleod. *Where are the others?*

* * *

Kirsten Stewart was raging inside. It didn't have to go down like that. Macleod had run forward, charged in to save someone. Save someone from themselves, initially, and then to save somebody else from being killed. It was nobody of importance. It was just Varney, one of them.

But Macleod was Macleod because he stood up for whatever person was there. Varney, clearly betrayed by the Forseti group, was about to die. Macleod had rushed to his aid.

Now, having secured the barn at quite a cost, for there were many who would not walk back out again, Kirsten was trying to hunt down the red hooded figure and Lady Cockburn.

She hadn't seen Macleod in the maze, but that was where the tunnel had emerged. Anna and she had split up, and Kirsten now walked quietly through the maze with her gun in front of her. Kirsten stole along, listening to the night. She couldn't hear anything but she spotted two figures.

She would have to be quick to catch them before they disappeared out the other end, for they might know the maze. Kirsten turned a corner. As she did so, she caught a flash of something. It had been a searchlight, a torch, something of that ilk. And she dived back across the hedge.

Kirsten heard the barest sound of a silenced gun. The bullet whipped into the hedge in front of her. She went to turn the other way into the passage that she'd come from, but she saw a figure in shadow at the far end. Kirsten slipped back to the slither of hedge in between the two passageways.

It wasn't protection, and she dropped to the ground on her bum, hearing silenced shots whistling past her ears. They were quiet, but they cut through the leaves leaving a quiet note in the night.

She would have to make a run for it. Right or left, she'd have to make a run for it. Kirsten withdrew her own gun and crouched down, waiting. She could hear them coming closer, hear them edging towards her. If she got tangled up with one, the other could come round the corner and kill her. She'd have to be quick.

Kirsten turned right, back into the corridor she'd come from, because that was the way she always turned best. As she did so, she was confronted by a man only three feet away, and she dived at him. He was blocking her, holding her up, their guns stuck in a jam together, and she twisted hers, slowly, desperate to get a shot off. She could see the man's delight, and then horror, and realised that someone must be behind her. Kirsten took a glance over her shoulder. She saw a man standing there with a gun.

'Just shoot her,' said the man she was engaged with. 'Shoot her.'

'I could hit you.'

'I said shoot her!'

'Okay, it's your funeral.'

Kirsten tried to force her hand to move out of the way, but then she heard a dull thud. Somebody fell to the ground behind her. The man she was engaged with looked stunned. Kirsten took her chance, manoeuvred her hand towards him, and snapped the man's neck. He dropped to the ground. Kirsten secured his gun before turning to see the other man lying, his gun in front of him. Behind him, she saw Clarissa, smiling.

'You okay, Kirstie?' she whispered.

Kirsten gave a nod, put her finger up to her lips, and then turned to continue back on the route she'd gone, stepping past Clarissa.

'Well, that's gratitude,' said Clarissa, quietly to herself. She picked up the other silenced gun that the man had dropped on falling and followed Kirsten.

* * *

Macleod turned a corner to find someone in his path. He jumped, went to attack them, but his hands were held. He then saw the face of Anna Hunt. Quietly, she said, 'Stick with me.'

'If we split, we can cover more ground,' said Macleod.

'If we split, you'll end up dead. Stick with me,' said Anna.

Anna crept forward at a speed that alarmed Macleod. He'd been going slowly, but maybe she knew better than he. Maybe she was trained to go at this pace. Did you surprise people more at speed when you arrived beside them? Macleod didn't know. All he knew was that Anna was moving fast, and he was struggling to keep up.

She darted past this hedge and that one and Macleod realised he was truly lost in this maze, but he could hear them. He could hear Lady Cockburn urging the other figure on. Anna went to a corner in the maze, stopped, and held her hand up to Macleod. She indicated he should watch behind her, down the passage they'd come. Macleod wondered exactly what he would do, for he had no gun.

She turned around the corner and then Macleod heard the cry. He thought he'd heard something. It wasn't a shot as such as they were usually a lot louder. But he carefully turned around the corner to see Anna lying on the ground. She'd been hit in the shoulder, he reckoned, or something akin, and she was looking back down the hedge-lined passage she was in.

A gun had fallen, and she'd been hit in the shoulder, causing her to lie prone. Someone was coming up close to her now. Macleod peered carefully and saw the man striding forward, his gun before him. It was a silenced one, for he could see the silencer barrel.

The man strode up quickly, held the gun out in front of him and Macleod realised he was going to kill Anna Hunt. He leapt from the hedge, surprising the man and knocking his hand off to the side. Two quiet bullets thudded into the ground.

The man pushed Macleod, and he hit the hedge behind him, before tumbling over somebody's feet. The man wheeled with the gun, but somebody was up and kicking him now. As his gun fell from the man's hands, Macleod saw a blur of black and the man dropped. Suddenly, Anna was crouching beside him.

'We need to move, Seoras. Thank you, but we need to move.'

She was off and he rolled himself to his feet, chasing her. As he watched, he could see that she'd slowed slightly. Wherever that bullet had gone, whatever it had done, it clearly was affecting her. He wondered that she hadn't cried out. Had it grazed her? Was it in there? He didn't know and he couldn't ask. Instead, they had to keep the hunt going?

* * *

Clarissa Urquhart had found a sundial in the maze. It wasn't a big one, although the plinth it was on came up to chest high. But the sundial on top, made of brass, wasn't attached to the plinth, but simply sat on it. Clarissa picked it up in her hand. It wasn't a bad size for wielding, and she knew she really needed a weapon at the moment.

Clarissa had picked up a gun with a silencer, but she wasn't sure she could use it. She wasn't sure if the safety would be on, because guns weren't her thing. She was walking along by a hedge when she saw in front of her two figures cross her path. One was in red, the other brown, with the hood down. It was Lady Cockburn.

Clarissa quickened her pace up. They'd turned round to

the left, and so she followed. By rights, she should have snuck round. By rights, she should have kept to a distance, protecting herself. But Clarissa was enraged. She'd had enough, more than enough, and was at boiling point.

She tore along down the hedge, turned again, and saw the couple desperately trying to edge away through their maze. Clarissa ran and threw the sundial when she was only a few feet behind. It caught Lady Cockburn in the back of the head, and the woman stumbled. The man in red looked to run, but Clarissa was up close now, and she leapt, throwing herself onto his back. She reached up and grabbed his hood.

The hood fell down, and Clarissa yanked the man's head round. It was Lord Cockburn. He spun, however, pushing her into the hedge, and with no purchase, she was unable to do anything except hold on to the man. She thrashed as best she could, but Lady Cockburn had got back up now, although still reeling.

She reached past her husband, planting a hand onto Clarissa's face. Scrabbling at the eyes forced Clarissa to defend herself. Both hands were flung up, grabbing at Lady Cockburn's hands, feeling the grip on them loosen. Lord Cockburn managed to drive an elbow into Clarissa's midriff. She gave a cry, and then tumbled down off the back of him. As she did so, Lady Cockburn stepped back. She reached inside her robe and pulled out a gun. Point blank, she looked down and gave a laugh. 'Urquhart,' she said, 'you so deserve this.'

Clarissa gulped, but as she did so, she saw Lady Cockburn fly back twice. She twisted this way and that, and then a third and a fourth time before falling to the floor. A shot was fired toward Lord Cockburn, but someone else had stepped into the fray now. And this newcomer, dressed like a security guard, whipped around and fell to the floor. When Clarissa looked again, Cockburn was gone. Clarissa was approached by Kirsten, who knelt down close beside her.

'Kirstie. Thank God, Kirstie. You saved me.'

'Stay down,' said Kirsten. 'I'll see if I can get him. You okay here?'

Clarissa gave a nod, but as Kirsten disappeared, she looked across. Lady Cockburn was lying on the floor, her head was twisted to one side, and a faint grin remained on the face. It made Clarissa shiver, and she wanted Kirsten to come back.

* * *

Macleod had heard shots, albeit silenced ones, ripping through the hedge. Having decided that he did not know where he was, he jumped up into the hedge and tried to climb it. He got up to the top, still lying on it to distribute his weight, but was able to see new figures approach. They'd gone right through the hedge line, up close to its entrance. And the new figures pulled weapons, firing towards the hedges.

There was gunfire coming back. But Macleod could see the red hooded figure, now with his hood down, running off towards a car. The car sped away, and Macleod saw the men who had run into the maze, now looking to fire up towards him. He rolled off the hedge, tumbling down into the maze below. He could hear more activity, on and off for the next five minutes. But with Cockburn gone, he holed himself up tighter now, making sure that he wouldn't give his presence away. Then someone appeared round the corner of the maze.

'You can get up now.' It was Anna Hunt.

'There's more men coming in,' he said. 'At the front of the

maze.'

'We've been there,' said Anna. 'It's sorted.' She was holding her shoulder.

'Did you get hit?'

'Flesh wound,' she said. 'It appears I owe you. Lady Cockburn's dead. Clarissa's okay.' She tapped the earpiece. 'Okay.' She confirmed with Perry that Sabine and he were still okay back at the barn. They said no one had been, and Anna advised that some of her team would come shortly. She then sat down on her bottom beside Macleod.

'It's over, Seoras. This is over.'

'But he got away,' said Macleod. 'How can it be over?' Anna put her hand up onto his shoulder.

'Trust me, Seoras. It's over.'

Chapter 25

Macleod had been to many funerals in his time as a serving police officer. He'd never got satisfaction from any of them. Some had been mundane, run-of-the-mill funerals for people who had died of natural causes. They were sad, but these things happened in life, and Macleod could manage them. The harder ones were for colleagues who died in the line of duty. Thankfully, there hadn't been that many. But here he was, watching the funeral of Lady Cockburn.

Beside him, Anna Hunt was dressed in black. Her hair was neatly brushed, and she wore a resolute grin on her face. Macleod wished death on no one, but he wondered if Anna had a different view. After all, she was sometimes called to take people out, stop them from committing their own atrocities in the most brutal of fashions. That was bound to change a person.

'Quite the pomp and ceremony,' said Macleod.

'I note Clarissa's here.'

'Yes,' said Macleod. 'She is. I think she just wants to make sure the woman's dead.'

'She did well,' said Anna. 'I don't want her on my team ever again. But she did well.'

'She walked away from the murder squad,' said Macleod. 'That's why I put her back in the arts. But she came face to face with it again. She never flinches. She just keeps going. Above all, she's a team player.'

'Sounds better than Rottweiler.'

'Oh, she's that,' said Macleod. 'That and more. You sure you don't want her?'

'Another week and Kirsten would have shot her,' said Anna. Macleod thought he would have burst out laughing, except it was such a sombre occasion.

Anna stayed with him to watch the entire funeral. As they walked away in the aftermath, mourners, many of whom were from high society, disappeared in chauffeured cars. Macleod wondered if he'd see Anna Hunt again in the near future.

'The Forseti group,' said Macleod. 'It's not done, is it? Cockburn got away. If he set it up once, he can set it up again.'

'We got all the arms, we just didn't get the head,' said Anna.

'But it could be done,' said Macleod. 'We've looked into it, more and more. Some of those who were injured, we've been able to get to talk. Lady Cockburn was the driving force behind it. Lord Cockburn was the figurehead, but she was the real brains. But they could start again.'

'I don't think you should worry yourself,' Anna said.

'Why?' asked Macleod.

'I said you had to identify who they were. You've identified them and have my thanks. You also saved my life, Seoras. I'm forever in your debt. You came to my aid when I couldn't trust anyone on my side. When my team was in difficulties and you never quit. I am grateful. And that's why I tell you, do not worry about Lord Cockburn.'

'I don't think I can be so sure,' said Macleod.

'Trust me,' said Anna. They got into Anna's car, and she drove Macleod back to his house on the Black Isle. Anna got out of the car with him and walked him to the door. 'Is Jane in?' she said.

'No, she's off out. Swimming, I think,' said Macleod. 'Do you want to come in? I can do you a drink or a cup of tea.' Anna turned and took Macleod's hand.

'The more I get to know you, Seoras, the more I want to say yes to that question. But you don't mean it how I'd like it. Be good. And if you ever bore of her, drop me a line. We'll go for a proper drink.'

The woman was outrageous, Macleod thought, and yet did it with style.

'I don't think that's going to be happening,' he said.

'No,' she said. 'That's why I said it. Take care of yourself. I'll miss our coffee, by Loch Ness, unless you come up with some other reason you need me.'

She reached forward and placed a kiss on his cheek. He stood and watched as she walked back to the car and then disappeared off. Before he met Jane, he might have been tempted. Then he corrected himself. Before he met Jane, he wouldn't have been anything. He was such a stuck-up fool. If Jane hadn't been here, yes, he would be tempted.

And that scared him, knowing who Anna Hunt was and what she did. Sometimes Macleod was cheered by his own growth and his progression. How he wasn't the same as he was before. But when he had thoughts like this with Anna Hunt, he wasn't sure he was wholly changed in the right direction. He turned, opened his front door, and stepped inside. He was going to sit down and have a proper rest.

* * *

Anna Hunt sighed as she parked the car up. She'd left it just outside the airport. In her head, she was kicking herself that there wasn't an available Seoras Macleod for her, to try to see if she could make something work. But this was her life, and she was about to have one of her more satisfying moments.

Anna disappeared inside a nearby hotel. Checking into her room, she found an outfit stolen from security at the airport. Twenty minutes later, Anna was at the security hut entering the airside of the airport, courtesy of a pass with her name on it.

A private jet was sitting right on the tarmac, and she recognised it. She spent some time around it, making sure no one else was watching, before disappearing over to one side and sitting by the perimeter edge.

A car pulled up beside the jet and for the merest of moments a man emerged and stepped onto the plane. Anna, on seeing him, reached down and pressed the button inside her pocket. She turned, walked away from the apron, back onto the land side and to the hotel where she changed again. Returning downstairs, she told reception she'd be checking out as, unfortunately, she had been called away on business.

Anna got into her car and drove before pulling up at a lay-by. She pulled out her laptop, positioned it on the passenger seat, and tapped in a few details before looking at the screen. It showed an aircraft getting airborne from Inverness Airport. It flew east and just as it cleared the land, it vanished from the screen. Anna sat back and smiled. Somewhere, two pieces of plane would be descending at speed into the sea. In one of them would be Lord Cockburn, and he wouldn't be coming back.

* * *

Macleod walked into the hospital at around about seven o'clock that evening. He'd just heard the news about the private jet which had exploded. They weren't sure how many were dead inside, and he shook his head at the bad luck. However, he was here for something good.

Jane was beside him, and hand in hand, they walked up to the maternity ward. He was pointed down to a day room, where, sitting in a hospital gown, was Hope McGrath. Her hair was splayed across her shoulders, and John was standing behind her. Macleod went over, but Hope pushed herself up, in obvious pain, from the wheelchair, and stepped awkwardly three or four steps to throw her arms around him. Macleod held her tight.

'You're safe, Seoras,' she said. 'You're safe.'

'You made it. You had me worried, girl. I was so worried.'

'She had us all worried,' said John.

'Is it over?' asked Hope.

'Anna told me it was. I don't know how, but she told me it was.'

'Good,' said Hope. Tears were welling from her eyes. 'We made it. We all made it. I went up to see Patterson today. He's okay. We knew he would be. And they said Jim's out of critical. He'll come back.'

'You saved his life,' said Macleod. 'You saved him. He owes you a lot.'

'For someone who once tried to kick me off the force, he's not bad.'

'I'm glad you can see it that way. How are you?'

'I'm sore. So very sore,' she said. 'They kicked me, beat me hard. John too.' Macleod could see the bruising around her face. No doubt the rest of her body was bruised, too. John was looking awkward. There was a cut underneath his eye. He seemed to be missing a tooth.

'But you made it,' said Macleod. Hope turned, half staggered back to her wheelchair, and sat down.

'I need you to come and meet someone,' she said.

'Do you want me to push you down to the ward?' asked John.

'Seoras, you push me. Do you mind, John? I just, I want to talk to Seoras. Is that okay, Jane?'

'Sure,' said Jane, 'Me and John will just have a good old chinwag.'

Macleod stepped forward and pushed Hope's wheelchair out of the dayroom. Behind him, he could hear Jane congratulating John.

'Down here, Seoras,' said Hope. Macleod continued to push her down the hall, but Hope told him to stop. 'Are you okay?' she asked.

'I don't think we'll be the same after this one,' he said. 'I can't do this. This one was, well, too much. We nearly lost so many people.'

'What are you saying?'

'I might call it quits soon, Hope. Jane gives up so much for me. And there I am, running around, risking my life. I had to send her away. It's endangering her too. I need to re-evaluate. I need to look at what's going on. But I won't do it until you're back. I need to be here for the team. Because as of now, you're on maternity.'

'I never felt so worried in my life. I never felt so vulnerable as a detective, Seoras. It's a good job I wasn't with you at the end. I'd have killed them.'

'I felt like that at times too,' said Macleod. 'The thought of losing you. Well . . .'

'I am coming back,' said Hope. 'John and I were talking about it before we were attacked. John's going to give up the hire-car firm. He wants to stay at home, says I need to keep going. He says it's in my blood. Even if I become a housewife and a mum, he says I'm a detective born and bred.'

'He's right,' said Macleod. 'And that's my worry if I quit. Will I have enough? As lovely as Jane is, will I still be hungering to come back?'

'Come on,' she said, 'getting too morbid. Down here.'

Macleod pushed her wheelchair down to a ward, pushed open the door, and they went inside to see two rows of cots. It was the ward for premature babies, a support unit to make sure that they got through the early days.

There was a nurse on duty who looked over and then smiled and said it was okay if they didn't make any noise. Hope pointed over to one of the far cots, and Macleod pushed her round. He knelt down beside her, as she leaned forward in her wheelchair.

'That's him, Seoras. That's my wee guy. He started off life with a beating, but he's tough. He's small, smaller than he should have been, but he's tough.'

'Like his mum, though I'm sure he'll grow to have your height.' Macleod put an arm around her, turned and kissed her on the cheek. 'Well done, mum. Well done. He's beautiful.'

'I want a godparent,' she said. 'In fact, I want two. You and Jane. I've also named him after you.'

Macleod's eyes were welling up now. 'Hello, little Seoras,' he said.

'Seoras? Don't be daft. I wouldn't dump something like that on the child.' Macleod looked at her, baffled. 'You need to welcome Ian John Macleod McGrath.'

'Macleod McGrath,' he smiled. 'If he's not a detective, I don't know what he's going to be.'

'At this moment in time, Seoras, I don't really care.'

Read on to discover the Patrick Smythe series!

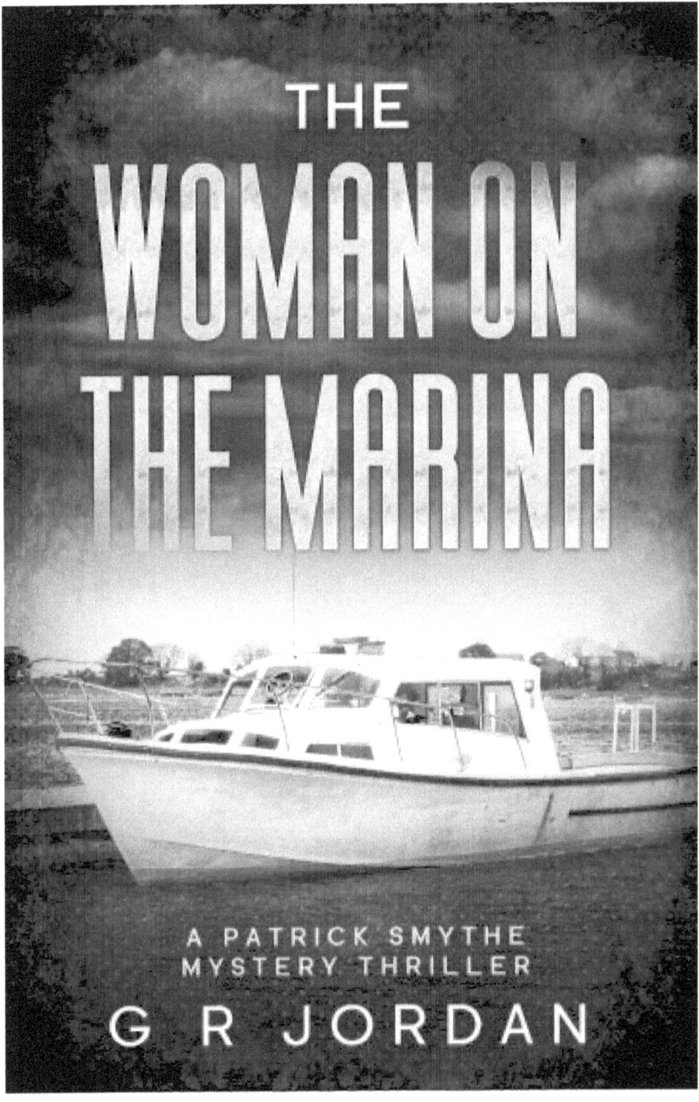

Patrick Smythe is a former Northern Irish policeman who after suffering an amputation after a bomb blast, takes to the sea between the west coast of Scotland and his homeland to ply his trade as a private investigator. Join Paddy as he tries to work to his own ethics while knowing how to bend the rules he once enforced. Working from his beloved motorboat 'Craigantlet', Paddy decides to rescue a drug mule in this short story from the pen of G R Jordan.

Join G R Jordan's monthly newsletter about forthcoming releases and special writings for his tribe of avid readers and then receive your free Patrick Smythe short story.

Go to https://bit.ly/PatrickSmythe for your Patrick Smythe journey to start

About the Author

GR Jordan is a self-published author who finally decided at forty that in order to have an enjoyable lifestyle, his creative beast within would have to be unleashed. His books mirror that conflict in life where acts of decency contend with self-promotion, goodness stares in horror at evil, and kindness blindsides us when we at our worst. Corrupting our world with his parade of wondrous and horrific characters, he highlights everyday tensions with fresh eyes whilst taking his methodical, intelligent mainstays on a roller-coaster ride of dilemmas, all the while suffering the banter of their provocative sidekicks.

A graduate of Loughborough University where he masqueraded as a chemical engineer but ultimately played American football, Gary had worked at changing the shape of cereal flakes and pulled a pallet truck for a living. Watching vegetables freeze at -40'C was another career highlight and he was also one of the Scottish Highlands "blind" air traffic controllers. These days he has graduated to answering a telephone to people in trouble before telephoning other people to sort it out.

Having flirted with most places in the UK, he is now based in the Isle of Lewis in Scotland where his free time is spent between raising a young family with his wife, writing, figuring out how to work a loom and caring for a small flock of chickens. Luckily, his writing is influenced by his varied work and life experience as the chickens have not been the poetical inspiration he had hoped for!

You can connect with me on:

https://grjordan.com

https://facebook.com/carpetlessleprechaun

Subscribe to my newsletter:

https://bit.ly/PatrickSmythe

Also by G R Jordan

G R Jordan writes across multiple genres including crime, dark and action adventure fantasy, feel good fantasy, mystery thriller and horror fantasy. Below is a selection of his work. Whilst all books are available across online stores, signed copies are available at his personal shop.

Mage of the Dice (Highlands & Islands Detective Book 47
https://grjordan.com/product/mage-of-the-dice
A deceased father of four, beheaded on a village green. A world-renowned game that starts a generational change. Can DI Emmett Grump roll the dice and find the long-forgotten killer amidst the geek millionaires?

When a die turns up as a missing piece of evidence in a long forgotten horrific death, DI Grump and DS Ferguson are tasked with finding the connection to a brutal beheading of a family man. As Grump goes deeper within his own beloved gaming world, he must come to terms with his once thought heroes as the villains of the peace. And when a company's future is at stake, Grump and Ferguson discover a games master can bring about the death of any character in the story.

A mage can roll the dice to whatever value he wants!

Kirsten Stewart Thrillers
https://grjordan.com/product/a-shot-at-democracy
Join Kirsten Stewart on a shadowy ride through the underbelly of the Highlands of Scotland where among the beauty and splendour of the majestic landscape lies corruption and intrigue to match any city. From murders to extortion, missing children to criminals operating above the law, the Highland former detective must learn a tougher edge to her work as she puts her own life on the line to protect those who cannot defend themselves.

Having left her beloved murder investigation team far behind, Kirsten has to battle personal tragedy and loss while adapting to a whole new way of executing her duties where your mistakes are your own. As Kirsten comes to terms with working with the new team, she often operates as the groups solo field agent, placing herself in danger and trouble to rescue those caught on the dark side of life. With action packed scenes and tense scenarios of murder and greed, the Kirsten Stewart thrillers will have you turning page after page to see your favourite Scottish lass home!

There's life after Macleod, but a whole new world of death!

Jac's Revenge (A Jac Moonshine Thriller #1)

https://grjordan.com/product/jacs-revenge

An unexpected hit makes Debbie a widow. The attention of her man's killer spawns a brutal yet classy alter ego. But how far can you play the game before it takes over your life?

All her life, Debbie Parlor lived in her man's shadow, knowing his work was never truly honest. She turned her head from news stories and rumours. But when he was disposed of for his smile to placate a rival crime lord, Jac Moonshine was born. And when Debbie is paid compensation for her loss like her car was written off, Jac decides that enough is enough.

Get on board with this tongue-in-cheek revenge thriller that will make you question how far you would go to avenge a loved one, and how much you would enjoy it!

A Giant Killing (Siobhan Duffy Mysteries #1)

https://grjordan.com/product/a-giant-killing

A body lies on the Giant's boot. Discord, as the master of secrets has been found. Can former spy Siobhan Duffy find the killer before they execute her former colleagues?

When retired operative Siobhan Duffy sees the killing of her former master in the paper, her unease sends her down a path of discovery and fear. Aided by her young housekeeper and scruff of a gardener, Siobhan begins a quest to discover the reason for her spy boss' death and unravels a can of worms today's masters would rather keep closed. But in a world of secrets, the difference between revenge and simple, if brutal, housekeeping becomes the hardest truth to know.

The past is a child who never leaves home!